THE QUOTABLE ROBERTSON DAVIES

THE QUOTABLE
ROBERTSON DAVIES

The Wit and Wisdom of the Master

Selected by

JAMES CHANNING SHAW

⟦A DOUGLAS GIBSON BOOK⟧

M&S

Library and Archives Canada Cataloguing in Publication

Davies, Robertson, 1913-1995
The quotable Robertson Davies : the wit and wisdom of the master / compiled by James Channing Shaw.

"A Douglas Gibson book".
ISBN 0-7710-8088-3

1. Davies, Robertson, 1913-1995 – Quotations. 2. Quotations, Canadian (English) I. Shaw, James Channing II. Title

PS8507.A67A6 2005   C813'.54   C2005-902186-1

We acknowledge the financial support of the Government of Canada through the Book Publishing Industry Development Program and that of the Government of Ontario through the Ontario Media Development Corporation's Ontario Book Initiative. We further acknowledge the support of the Canada Council for the Arts and the Ontario Arts Council for our publishing program.

Typeset in Garamond by M&S, Toronto
Printed and bound in Canada

This book is printed on acid-free paper that is 100% recycled, ancient-forest friendly (100% post-consumer recycled).

A Douglas Gibson Book

McClelland & Stewart Ltd.
The Canadian Publishers
481 University Avenue
Toronto, Ontario
M5G 2E9
www.mcclelland.com

1 2 3 4 5   09 08 07 06 05

Contents

Preface

Robertson Davies had a talent for distilling human experience into quotable literary gems. He was a master of truisms. From the time of my discovery of Robertson Davies's writing, some of my greatest pleasures in reading Davies's work have come from his quotable aphorisms, opinions, and general advice for living. The quotations, usually no more than one sentence in length, address most of the important issues in life: faith, love, men, women, art, literature, life itself. Some quotation-worthy phrases are mere descriptions beautifully composed, or opinions about Canadian life, or a humorously irreverent insult. In Davies's novels and plays there is an abundance of these passages, with many more in his critical writing and in the Samuel Marchbanks books.

This collection of approximately eight hundred quotations was selected from Davies's written works. Those expressed in the spoken words of Davies's characters are labelled with the character's name in parentheses. Some are identified as the thoughts of the narrator. The quotations from Samuel Marchbanks, the fictional alter-ego of Robertson Davies, are labelled by book title. All are quintessential Robertson Davies.

Enjoy!

James Channing Shaw

Academia / University Life

You can always date an academic by the cut of his dress suit, which he buys before he is thirty and uses very sparingly for the next forty-five years. — *High Spirits*

Ah, that blessed degree that stamps us for life as creatures of guaranteed intellectual worth.
— (John Parlabane) *The Rebel Angels*

Judge a man by what he publishes, not by what he hides in a bottom drawer. — (Professor Stromwell) *The Rebel Angels*

The characteristic of the artist is discontent. Universities may produce fine critics, but not artists. We are wonderful people, we university people, but we are apt to forget the limitations of learning, which cannot create or beget.
— (Professor Hitzig) *The Rebel Angels*

However much science and educational theory and advanced thinking you pump into a college or a university, it always retains a strong hint of its medieval origins . . .
— (Simon Darcourt, narr.) *The Rebel Angels*

We knew all about the meetings where anxious deans fluttered and fussed to make sure that every shade of opinion was heard, and strangled decisive action in the slack, dusty ropes of academic scruple.
— (Simon Darcourt, narr.) *The Rebel Angels*

Scientists are what universities produce best and oftenest. Science is discovery and revelation, and that is not art.
— (Professor Hitzig) *The Rebel Angels*

The energy of the modern university lives in the love affair between government and science, and sometimes the two are so close it makes you shudder.
— (Simon Darcourt, narr.) *The Rebel Angels*

It is quite extraordinary what charity universities extend toward people who have known the great. It's a form of romanticism, I suppose. Any wandering Englishman who remembers Virginia Woolf, or Wyndham Lewis, or E.M. Forster can pick up a fee and eat and drink himself paralytic in any university on this continent.
— (Professor Durdle) *The Rebel Angels*

Scholars are mendicants. Always have been, and always will be – or so I hope. God help us all if they ever got control of any real money. – (Professor Czermak) *The Rebel Angels*

Academicism runs in the blood like syphilis.
– (Professor Czermak) *The Rebel Angels*

Paleo-psychology: It's really digging into what people thought, in times when their thinking was a muddle of religion and folk-belief and rags of misunderstood classical learning, instead of being what it is today, which I suppose you'd have to call a muddle of materialism, and folk-belief, and rags of misunderstood scientific learning.
– (Maria Theotoky) *The Rebel Angels*

Universities cannot be more universal than the people who teach, and the people who learn, within their walls. Those who can get beyond the fashionable learning of their day are few. – (Simon Darcourt, narr.) *The Rebel Angels*

In a university you cannot get rid of a tenured professor without an unholy row, and though academics love bickering they hate rows. – (Simon Darcourt, narr.) *The Rebel Angels*

I take refuge in the scholar's disclaimer . . . it's not my field.
– (Urquhart McVarish) *The Rebel Angels*

Energy and curiosity are the lifeblood of universities; the desire to find out, to uncover, to dig deeper, to puzzle out obscurities, is the spirit of the university, and it is a channelling of that unresting curiosity that holds mankind together. As for energy, only those who have never tried it for a week or two can suppose that the pursuit of knowledge does not demand a strength and determination, a resolve not to be beaten, that is a special kind of energy, and those who lack it or have it only in small store will never be scholars or teachers, because real teaching demands energy as well. To instruct calls for energy, and to remain almost silent, but watchful and helpful, while students instruct themselves, calls for even greater energy. To see someone fall (which will teach him not to fall again) when a word from you would keep him on his feet but ignorant of an important danger, is one of the tasks of the teacher that calls for special energy, because holding in is more demanding than crying out. — (Simon Darcourt, narr.) *The Rebel Angels*

Universities were creations of the Middle Ages, and much of the Middle Ages still clings to them, not only in their gowns and official trappings, but deep in their hearts. — (Professor Archey Deloney) *The Rebel Angels*

You call yourself a scholar! Haven't you learned rule number one of scholarship: *never, under any circumstances, throw anything away?* — (Simon Darcourt) *The Lyre of Orpheus*

A tenured professor could commit the Sin Against the Holy Ghost and get away with it, if he could find the right lawyer. — *The Lyre of Orpheus*

The professor who does not leave his campus knows that no complete abandonment of responsibility is possible.
— *The Lyre of Orpheus*

Art is always in peril at universities, where there are so many people, young and old, who love art less than argument, and dote upon a text that provides the nutritious pemmican on which scholars love to chew.
— (Dr. Jonathan Hullah, narr.) *The Cunning Man*

Money is a great cushion against academic failure.
— (Dr. Jonathan Hullah, narr.) *The Cunning Man*

If you start with a preconceived idea of what you are going to find, you are liable to find it, and be dead wrong, and maybe miss something genuine that's under your nose.
— (Professor Ozias Froats) *The Rebel Angels*

Scholars, like hens, must lay eggs at regular intervals if they expect anyone to keep them.
— (Professor Idris Rowlands) *Fortune, My Foe*

The beauty of ethics is that nobody can be perfectly certain about what it includes or even what it means.
— (Conor Gilmartin, narr.) *Murther & Walking Spirits*

Nowadays, of course, all professors are funny; it has been made clear to them that they are a special branch of the entertainment world; if they are not amusing, their students will not become involved with what they are teaching, and a professor whose students are not involved is a man in deep and probably irremediable disgrace.
— *One Half of Robertson Davies*

Nowadays the only professors permitted to be wholly serious are those so eminent that they have become, in effect, walking monuments to their own intellectual splendour. — *One Half of Robertson Davies*

On a professor's salary large-scale vice is out of the question.
— *One Half of Robertson Davies*

The aspirant to academic perfection so immerses himself in the works of his god that he inevitably takes on something of his quality, at least in externals. It is not the fault of the god. Not at all. — *One Half of Robertson Davies*

Art

If you fill the world with common sense, there'll be precious little art left. Art begins where common sense leaves off.
— (Peggy Stamper) *A Mixture of Frailties*

Nothing, nothing whatever really stands in the way of a creative artist except lack of talent.
— (Sir Benedict Domdaniel) *A Mixture of Frailties*

If formal education has any bearing on the arts at all, its purpose is to make critics, not artists. Its usual effect is to cage the spirit in other people's ideas — the ideas of poets and philosophers, which were once splendid insights into the nature of life, but which people who have no insights of their own have hardened into dogmas.
— (Signor Sacchi) *A Mixture of Frailties*

If you want to attract real, serious attention to your work, you can't beat being dead.
— (Bun Eccles) *A Mixture of Frailties*

Extraordinary how people sometimes create so much better than they live.
— (Sir Benedict Domdaniel) *A Mixture of Frailties*

Film is like painting, which is also unchanging. But each viewer brings his personal sensibility, his unique response to the complete canvas as he does to the film.
— (Jurgen Lind) *World of Wonders*

Amateur photography bears the same relation to the real thing that amateur theatricals bear to the productions of London or Broadway. — *The Diary of Samuel Marchbanks*

Provincial critics are always cool: they have to show they're not impressed by what comes from the big centres of culture. — (Magnus Eisengrim, narr.) *World of Wonders*

The half-Catholics are not meant to be artists, any more than the half-anything-elses.
— (Tancred Saraceni) *What's Bred in the Bone*

A portrait is, among other things, a statement of opinion by the artist, as well as a "likeness," which is what everybody wants it to be. — *What's Bred in the Bone*

Catholicism has begotten much great art; Protestantism none at all – not a single painting. But Catholicism has fostered art in the very teeth of Christianity. The Kingdom of Christ, if it ever comes, will contain no art; Christ never showed the least concern with it. His church has inspired much but not because of anything the Master said. Who then was the inspirer? The much-maligned Devil, one supposes. It is he who understands and ministers to man's carnal and intellectual self, and art is carnal and intellectual.

— (Tancred Saraceni) *What's Bred in the Bone*

Artists have tunnel vision. They see what they are doing themselves, and they are plagued by all sorts of self-doubt and misgivings. Only the critic can stand aloof and see what's really going on. Only the critic is in a position to make a considered and sometimes a final judgment.

— (Alwyn Ross) *What's Bred in the Bone*

If life is a dream, as some philosophers insist, surely the great picture is that which most potently symbolizes the unseizable reality that lies behind the dream.

— (Tancred Saraceni) *What's Bred in the Bone*

Art is a cruel obsession.

— (Tancred Saraceni) *What's Bred in the Bone*

Too many fingers in pies are the utter ruin of art and the curse of drama. — (ETAH in Limbo) *The Lyre of Orpheus*

Raw heart can't make art but woe to art when it snubs heart.

— (Geraint Powell) *The Lyre of Orpheus*

In the world of art you never know who knows or has known who, and what is personal and what is derivative. That's part of the misery of the lesser artist. People think they copy, whereas they really just think the same way as somebody bigger, but not as effectively.

— (Darcy Dwyer) *The Cunning Man*

The worst artistic tragedy is not to be a failure, but just to fall short of the kind of success you have marked as your own. — (Hugh McWearie) *The Cunning Man*

I might have been an artist. But I played safe and became a teacher. That's fatal. Contact with the young and their perpetual curiosity soon kills the spark in a man. Teaching means forever going back to the beginning again. An artist must press on. — (Professor Idris Rowlands) *Fortune, My Foe*

Art, if it is to be great art, must be created afresh every time for the special group that has gathered to experience it.

— *One Half of Robertson Davies*

Those who claim to experience and value art only on the highest level know nothing whatever about art.

— *One Half of Robertson Davies*

Art is not democratic; it is aristocratic, and to suggest that everybody will love the highest when they see it is

demonstrably rubbish. They won't. But they will love what
reaches them. — *One Half of Robertson Davies*

Art, I am utterly convinced, is one of the principal roads by
which we find our way to such knowledge of this world and
the Universe to which it belongs as may be possible to us.
— *One Half of Robertson Davies*

Beauty

Beauty is in a great degree the art of suggestion.
— *Renown at Stratford*

Quietness is a great beautifier. — *Tempest-Tost*

Biography

Biography at its best is a form of fiction. — *The Lyre of Orpheus*

The scruples of a biographer are peculiar to the trade.
— *The Lyre of Orpheus*

Books

Nothing is more fatal to maidenly delicacy of speech than the run of a good library. — *Tempest-Tost*

Anything which concerns a subject dear to us seems to leap from a large page of print. — *Tempest-Tost*

The better a book is, the less money it will make.
— (Professor Idris Rowlands) *Fortune, My Foe*

It takes a man already wise to learn further wisdom from a book. — *A Voice from the Attic*

A book is good in relation to its reader. — *A Voice from the Attic*

There was a time when reformers thought that if education were available to the masses, the masses would love it, and every humble cottage would be bursting at the seams with cheap reprints of the world's classics. In this supposition, as in many another, the reformers were somewhat optimistic. A real dictatorship of the proletariat — if such a thing existed — would quickly result in a bookless world.
— *The Diary of Samuel Marchbanks*

Real bibliophiles do not put their books on shelves for people to look at or handle. They have no desire to show off their darlings, or to amaze people with their possessions. They keep their prized books hidden away in a secret spot to which they resort stealthily, like a Caliph visiting his harem, or a church elder sneaking into a bar. To be a book-collector is to combine the worst characteristics of a dope-fiend with those of a miser. — *The Table Talk of Samuel Marchbanks*

A book is criticized by the reviewer in direct proportion as the reviewer is criticized by the book: no man can find wisdom in print which is not already waiting for words within himself. — *Samuel Marchbanks' Almanack*

Boredom

Boredom is rich soil for every kind of rancour and ugliness. — (Magnus Eisengrim, narr.) *World of Wonders*

Boredom and stupidity and patriotism, especially when combined, are three of the greatest evils of the world we live in. — (Magnus Eisengrim, narr.) *World of Wonders*

Business

Too much attention to the details of business can be as bad as too little. – (Conor Gilmartin, narr.) *Murther & Walking Spirits*

He had in the highest degree the superior businessman's ability to delegate responsibility without relinquishing significant power. – *The Lyre of Orpheus*

Canada

Canada . . . the Home of Modified Rapture.
– (Penny) *The Lyre of Orpheus*

We are devil-worshippers, we Canadians, half in love with easeful Death. We flog ourselves endlessly, as a kind of spiritual purification. – (Solomon Bridgetower) *Tempest-Tost*

Why do countries have to have literatures? Why does a country like Canada, so late upon the international scene, feel that it must rapidly acquire the trappings of older countries – music of its own, pictures of its own, books of its own – and why does it fuss and stew and storm the heavens with its outcries when it does not have them?
– (Solomon Bridgetower) *Leaven of Malice*

A superstitious belief persists in Canada that nothing of importance can be done in the summer. The sun, which exacts the uttermost from nature, seems to have a numbing effect upon the works of man. — *A Mixture of Frailties*

In Canada we geld everything, if we can.
— (David Staunton, narr.) *The Manticore*

I think we are foolish on this continent to imagine that after five hundred generations somewhere else we become wholly Canadian — hard-headed, no-nonsense North Americans — in the twinkling of a single life.
— (John Parlabane) *The Rebel Angels*

Whoever lives in the finest house in a small Canadian town dwells in a House of Atreus, about which a part of the community harbours the darkest mythical suspicions. Sycophancy is present, but in small store; it is jealousy, envy, detraction, and derision that proliferate. In lesser houses there may be fighting, covert abortions, children "touched up" with a hot flat-iron to make them obedient, every imaginable aspect of parsimony, incest, and simple, persistent cruelty, but these are nothing to whatever seems amiss at the Big House. It is the great stage of its town, on which are played out the dramas that grip the imagination for years after the actors are dead, or have assumed new roles. — *What's Bred in the Bone*

For a lot of good reasons, including some strong planetary influences, Canada is an introverted country straining like hell to behave like an extrovert.
— (Ruth Nibsmith) *What's Bred in the Bone*

Ottawa is not a place to which anyone goes at the end of November simply for pleasure. — *The Lyre of Orpheus*

[Canada], the little country with the big body, which had always been introverted in its psychology — an introversion that had shown itself in a Loyalist bias, a refusal to be liberated by the military force of its mighty neighbour from what the mighty neighbour assumed was an intolerable colonial yoke — was striving now to assume the extroversion of that mighty neighbour. Because Canada could not really understand the American extroversion, it imitated the obvious elements in it, and the effect was often tawdry. Canada had lost its way, had suffered what anthropologists call Loss of Soul. But when the Soul was such a doubting, flickering, shy entity, who would regret its loss when there were big, obvious, and immediate gains to be had?
— *What's Bred in the Bone*

We cannot take our place in the world as a nation of millions of hockey-watchers and a few score hockey-players.
— (Alwyn Ross) *What's Bred in the Bone*

The mainspring of a Canadian's patriotism is not love, but duty. — (Nicholas Hayward) *Fortune, My Foe*

Sometimes for us in Canada it seems as though the United States and the United Kingdom were cup and saucer, and Canada the spoon, for we are in and out of both with the greatest freedom, and we are given most recognition when we are most a nuisance. — *A Voice from the Attic*

The plain fact is that most Canadians dislike and mistrust any great show of cheerfulness.
— *The Diary of Samuel Marchbanks*

Consumption, cancer, and the pox are all said to be on the increase in this country, but in my opinion the disease of bad manners is outstripping them all.
— *The Diary of Samuel Marchbanks*

What horse racing is to Irishmen, or singing contests to Welshmen, politics is to the Canadian.
— *The Diary of Samuel Marchbanks*

The true Canadian can be brought back from the grave, lured from his treasure chest or beguiled from his mistress' bower by two things — an argument about religion or an argument about politics. — *The Diary of Samuel Marchbanks*

Painted some verandah furniture this afternoon, so that when summer comes I shall be ready to enjoy all four hours of it. — *The Diary of Samuel Marchbanks*

What I always say about Canadian climate is that it saves us millions of dollars in travel; we can freeze with the Eskimo or sweat with the Zulu, or parch with the Arab, or drench with the Briton, and all in our own front gardens. Sometimes we even have some really beautiful weather, but not often enough to spoil us. — *The Diary of Samuel Marchbanks*

"Not Original, But Faithful To Death" is our motto in matters of humour. We like a joke to go off in our faces, like an exploding cigar, and then we can laugh heartily and get back to glum platitudes again. This characteristic is particularly noticeable in Parliament.
— *The Diary of Samuel Marchbanks*

All works and too few plays makes Canada a dull nation.
— *The Table Talk of Samuel Marchbanks*

There comes a time in every man's life when he wants to tell somebody who is pestering him to go to hell, and if he does not indulge the whim he is likely to get psychic strabismus, which, in its turn, leads to spiritual impotence. And spiritual impotence is the curse of our country as it is.
— *The Diary of Samuel Marchbanks*

Acceptance of the full gamut of human experience, from high to low, is greatly feared by a substantial number of Canadians. — *The Table Talk of Samuel Marchbanks*

In Canada anyone is respectable who does no obvious harm to his fellow man, and who takes care to be very solemn, and disapproving toward those who are not solemn.
— *The Table Talk of Samuel Marchbanks*

What a wonderful thing it is to see an Ontario audience laugh! Those stony, disapproving, thin-lipped faces, eloquent of our bitter winters, our bitter politics, and our bitter religion, melt into unaccustomed merriment, and a sense of relief is felt all through the theatre, as though the straps and laces of a tight corset had been momentarily loosened. — *The Table Talk of Samuel Marchbanks*

Nobody is interested in Canadians except, very occasionally, other Canadians. — *Samuel Marchbanks' Almanack*

If I had the management of Hell I should arrange for it to be a place where everybody had to sit on kitchen chairs, in a bad light, at a temperature of about forty-five degrees Fahrenheit, reading the Canada Gazette. A few aeons of that would show sinners what was what.
— *Samuel Marchbanks' Almanack*

. . . that special architectural picturesqueness which is only to be found in Canada, and which is more easily found in Salterton than in newer Canadian cities. Now the peculiar quality of this picturesqueness does not lie in a superficial resemblance to the old world; it is, rather, a compound of colonialism, romanticism, and sturdy defiance of taste; it is a fascinating and distinguished ugliness which is best observed in the light of Canadian November and December afternoons. This picturesqueness is not widely admired, and examples of it are continually being destroyed, without one voice being raised in their defence. But where they exist, and are appreciated, they suggest a quality which is rather that of Northern Europe – of Scandinavia and pre-revolutionary Russia – than of England or the U.S.A. It is in such houses as these that the characters in the plays of Ibsen had their being; it was in this light and against these backgrounds of stained wood and etched glass that the people of Tchekov talked away their lives. And, if the Canadian building be old enough, the perceptive eye may see faint ghosts from Pushkin and Lermontov moving through the halls. This is the architecture of a Northern people, upon which the comfort of England and the luxury of the United States have fallen short of their full effect. – *Leaven of Malice*

Cleanliness is the bugbear of this continent, and too much is sacrificed to it. – *The Table Talk of Samuel Marchbanks*

Montreal still holds her head high, but has bags under her eyes and wears mended stockings.
— *The Table Talk of Samuel Marchbanks*, editorial comment, 1985

I always think of Toronto as a big fat rich girl who has lots of money, but no idea of how to make herself attractive. She has not learned to drink like a lady, and she has not learned to laugh easily; when she does laugh, she shows the roof of her mouth; she is dowdy and mistakes dowdiness for a guarantee of virtue. She is neither a jolly country girl with hay in her hair, like many other Ontario cities, nor is she a delicious wanton, like Montreal; she is irritatingly conscious of her own worthiness. . . . Toronto ought to read the advertisements which explain why girls are unpopular and get themselves whispered about. Maybe she needs more bulk in her diet. — *The Table Talk of Samuel Marchbanks*

Celtic

A Celtic temperament; a difficult heritage.
— (The Lesser Zadkiel) *What's Bred in the Bone*

As a Celt, I am at once credulous of everything and skeptical of everything, and not a whole-hogger, who rushes from Mother of God to Mary Baker Eddy, and from her to LSD,

expecting some revelation that will settle everything. I don't want everything settled. I enjoy the mess.
— *Samuel Marchbanks' Almanack*

Character

Popularity and good character are not related.
— (Dunstan Ramsay, narr.) *Fifth Business*

People only get chances if they're ready for them. It's not luck. It's character. — (George Medwall) *A Mixture of Frailties*

Smug people say that character is destiny; they might say with equal sense that destiny is character.
— (Professor Idris Rowlands) *Fortune, My Foe*

Our real character — witty, ebullient, laughter-loving — doesn't matter: it's the publicity that counts.
— *Samuel Marchbanks' Almanack*

Character lies deeper than any question of psychosomatic medicine, and contains the key to cure — or at least to courageous endurance.
— (Dr. Jonathan Hullah, narr.) *The Cunning Man*

Children

It is never easy for children to defend their friends against disapproving parents. — *A Mixture of Frailties*

If there is one thing which utterly destroys a boy's character, it is to be needed. Boys are unendurable unless they are wholly expendable. — (Humphrey Cobbler) *Tempest-Tost*

All real fantasy is serious. Only faked fantasy is not serious. That is why it is so wrong to impose faked fantasy on children. — (Dr. J. von Haller) *The Manticore*

Children hear far more than people think, and understand much, if not everything.
— (David Staunton, narr.) *The Manticore*

Children do not question their destiny. Indeed, children do not live their lives; their lives, on the contrary, live them.
— (David Staunton, narr.) *The Manticore*

An infant is a seed. Is it an oak seed or a cabbage seed? Who knows? All mothers think their children are oaks but the world never lacks for cabbages. I would be the last man to pretend that knowing somebody as a child gave any real clue to who he is as a man.
— (Dunstan Ramsay) *World of Wonders*

What really shapes and conditions and makes us is somebody only a few of us ever have the courage to face: and that is the child you once were, long before formal education ever got its claws into you – that impatient, all demanding child who wants love and power and can't get enough of either and who goes on raging and weeping in your spirit till at last your eyes are closed and all the fools say, "Doesn't he look peaceful?" It is those pent-up, craving children who make all the wars and all the horrors and all the art and all the beauty and discovery in life, because they are trying to achieve what lay beyond their grasp before they were five years old. – (John Parlabane) *The Rebel Angels*

Christmas is best for children, and for those who are growing old; in the middle life one's capacity for enjoyment is under the constraint of a thousand responsibilities.
– *The Table Talk of Samuel Marchbanks*

Whoever declares a child to be "delicate" thereby crowns and anoints a tyrant. – *The Cunning Man*

Children often underestimate what their parents can grasp.
– (Maria Theotoky) *The Rebel Angels*

A happy childhood has spoiled many a promising life.
– (The Daimon Maimas) *What's Bred in the Bone*

Who ever knows what children hear and make their own forever? – (Conor Gilmartin, narr.) *Murther & Walking Spirits*

You'd be surprised how early the distinctive strain asserts itself in a really good young mind.
– (Dr. Jonathan Hullah, narr.) *The Cunning Man*

I am of the firm opinion that Shakespeare in printed form should be kept from children; if they cannot meet him in the theatre, better not meet him at all. One might just as well ask children to read the symphonies of Beethoven.
– (Dr. Jonathan Hullah, narr.) *The Cunning Man*

It's a wise child that knows its own father. – *High Spirits*

Everybody likes children – more or less – but most people can, at very infrequent intervals, get enough of them.
– *One Half of Robertson Davies*

A century ago a child expected to be beaten, pinched, shaken, cuffed, locked in dark cupboards, bastinadoed, and told it would go to Hell all day and every day, even in the happiest homes. And with what result? They grew up to be the Gladstones, Huxleys, Darwins, Tennysons, and other Great Victorians whom we all admire. Nowadays, with our weak-kneed kindness, we are raising a generation of nincompoops and clodhoppers. – *The Diary of Samuel Marchbanks*

Of all created creatures, there is surely none capable of such bone-headed, thoughtless cruelty as a healthy growing boy.
— *The Diary of Samuel Marchbanks*

Children invent magic; later in life we are still subject to this sway, but we invent "scientific" theories, and "philosophies" to make it intellectually respectable.
— *The Diary of Samuel Marchbanks*

Children never forgive their elders for their ignorance. It is obviously a grown-up's business to know.
— *The Table Talk of Samuel Marchbanks*

Tories, that's what children are, perpetuating the same old nonsense from generation to generation.
— *The Table Talk of Samuel Marchbanks*

What is the use of a large vocabulary of words, if the child has only a small range of ideas?
— *The Table Talk of Samuel Marchbanks*

The fashion in scientific horrors may change, but the witches will go on, and on, chasing generations of horror-stricken children down the shadowy labyrinths of sleep.
— *The Table Talk of Samuel Marchbanks*

Children are becoming a luxury beyond the reach of all but the affluent. What has become of the Old-Fashioned Child that slept on straw and was grateful for a bowl of table-leavings once a day? The Family Unit totters!
— *Samuel Marchbanks' Almanack*

Civilization

Civilization rests on two things . . . the discovery that fermentation produces alcohol, and voluntary ability to inhibit defecation. — (Professor Hitzig) *The Rebel Angels*

The Americans are to the civilization of our day what the Romans were to the civilization of the ancient world: they are its middle-men, its popularizers, not its creators.
— (Professor Idris Rowlands) *Fortune, My Foe*

The more complex our civilization becomes, the less fun there is in it and the more work there is to do.
— *The Diary of Samuel Marchbanks*

Cliché

We must remember that things become clichés because they are of frequent occurrence, and powerful impact.
— *One Half of Robertson Davies*

The blessing that children bring is a cliché. It is as corny as the rhymes of Ella Wheeler Wilcox about art. But one of the most difficult tasks for the educated and sophisticated mind is to recognize that some clichés are also important truths.
— *The Lyre of Orpheus*

It is cliché that the birth of a child is a symbol of hope, however disappointed and distressed that hope may at last prove to be. The baptism is a ceremony in which that hope is announced, and Hope is one of the knightly virtues.
— *The Lyre of Orpheus*

Critics

It is the first aim of the virtuoso not to please critics, but to awe them into silence and acceptance. This is another way of meeting the requirements of art. Critics define but do not advance the boundaries of art, which is what the virtuoso seeks to do. — *The Mirror of Nature*

[Critics] attempt to deal with the performances of artists who have spent not less than ten years acquiring insight and a formidable technique, in a maimed and cretinous prose which could not possibly give anybody any impression except one of confusion and depleted vitality. They are poor grammarians, and their vocabularies are tawdry. It is hard enough to interpret one art in terms of another under the best of circumstances, but when the critic has not understood that writing also is an art, his criticism becomes embarrassing self-portraiture.
— *Samuel Marchbanks' Almanack*

Curiosity

Curiosity is part of the cement that holds society together.
— *High Spirits*

When a man loses his curiosity he has lost the thing which binds him to humanity.
— (Professor Idris Rowlands) *Fortune, My Foe*

Cynicism

If one becomes a cynic about oneself the next step is the physical suicide which is the other half of that form of self-destruction. — (Magnus Eisengrim, narr.) *World of Wonders*

Cynicism, like all attitudes of mind, receives as much colour from the man who assumes it as it gives to him.
— *A Voice from the Attic*

Indigestion is a great begetter of cynicism. — *The Lyre of Orpheus*

Death

Ghosts are all rampaging egotists — forces of egotism that refuse to accept death as a fact. — *High Spirits*

She was experiencing that intoxicating upsurge of energy some women have when their husbands die.
— (Maria Theotoky) *The Rebel Angels*

To be robbed of the dignity of a natural death is a terrible deprivation. — (Maria Theotoky) *The Rebel Angels*

Death, though people prate about its universality, is doubtless individual in the way it comes to everyone.
— *What's Bred in the Bone*

It is a firm critical principle that nobody living is quite as good as somebody dead. — *The Lyre of Orpheus*

Failure to succeed in suicide is the ultimate ignominy.
— *The Diary of Samuel Marchbanks*

Beware of an optimism founded on superficial judgments: otherwise you will dismiss Death as Nature's bounty toward the undertaking industry. — *Samuel Marchbanks' Almanack*

The Devil

The Devil is a fine craftsman, and so many of his arguments are unanswerable.
— (Conor Gilmartin, narr.) *Murther & Walking Spirits*

The Devil knows corners of us all of which Christ Himself is ignorant. — (Padre Blazon) *Fifth Business*

Doctors

Nobody who is not at least equally loaded with science and arcane knowledge likes to criticize a doctor. Doctors rank just below parsons in their special sanctity.
— (Conor Gilmartin, narr.) *Murther & Walking Spirits*

Doctors do not always know what is going on in the mind of a patient, and there can be great fear of death when experiencing something which does not, in truth, bring death close. — (Dr. Jonathan Hullah, narr.) *The Cunning Man*

The physician is the priest of our modern, secular world.
— (Dr. Jonathan Hullah, narr.) *The Cunning Man*

A doctor's treatment is always a reflection of himself, to some degree. — (Inge Christofferson) *The Cunning Man*

[Medicine] is a profession of compassion, and when compassion does not arise naturally it must be faked.
— (Dr. Jonathan Hullah, narr.) *The Cunning Man*

Too many doctors are deeply interested in disease, but don't care much for people. — *The Diary of Samuel Marchbanks*

Education

Education in England spoils so many Canadians – except Rhodes scholars, who come back and get Government jobs right away. – (Mrs. Roscoe Forrester) *Tempest-Tost*

The determination of the man who works his way through the university is beyond question, but it is not likely that he will get as much from his experience as the student more fortunately placed. He has not time to be young, or to invite his soul. – *Tempest-Tost*

If a boy can't have a good teacher, give him a psychological cripple or an exotic failure to cope with; don't just give him a bad, dull teacher. – (Dunstan Ramsay, narr.) *Fifth Business*

He is not inhibited by education which is the great modern destroyer of truth and originality.
– (Dr. Liselotte Naegeli) *World of Wonders*

Education is a great shield against experience. It offers so much, ready-made and all from the best shops, that there's a temptation to miss your own life in pursuing the lives of your betters. It makes you wise in some ways, but it can make you a blindfolded fool in others.
– (Magnus Eisengrim, narr.) *World of Wonders*

I have often been amazed at how well comfortable and even rich people understand the physical deprivations of the poor, without having any notion of their intellectual squalor, which is one of the things that makes them miserable. It's a squalor that is bred in the bone, and rarely can education do much to root it out if education is simply a matter of schooling.

— (Magnus Eisengrim, narr.) *World of Wonders*

If you're going to be a genius you should try either to avoid education entirely, or else work hard to get rid of any you've been given. Education is for commonplace people and it fortifies their commonplaceness. Makes them useful, of course, in an ordinary sort of way.

— (Magnus Eisengrim, narr.) *World of Wonders*

[A university] is not a river to be fished, it's an ocean in which the young should bathe, and give themselves up to the tides and the currents.

— (John Parlabane) *The Rebel Angels*

Education is not an answer to anything, unless it is united to some basic endowment of common sense, goodness of heart, and recognition of the brotherhood of mankind . . .

— (Professor Ludlow) *The Rebel Angels*

How much more complicated life is than the attainment of a Ph.D. would lead one to believe!
— (Maria Theotoky) *The Rebel Angels*

Education makes a greater gulf in families even than making a lot of money. — *What's Bred in the Bone*

He knew what "aesthetic" meant; but it was plain from the way it was said that an "ESSthete" was a pretty feeble chap, wasting his time on art when he ought to be building up his character and facing the realities of life – as the hostile masters, failures to a man, understood life.
— *What's Bred in the Bone*

Schools, since their beginning, have been devised to keep children out of their parents' way, and in our time they have the added economic duty of keeping able-bodied young folk off the labour market.
— (Dr. Jonathan Hullah, narr.) *The Cunning Man*

A boy who can go through a first-rate boarding-school and emerge in one piece is ready for most of what the world is likely to bring him.
— (Dr. Jonathan Hullah, narr.) *The Cunning Man*

If I were successful, I would enter on university work without having to do the obligatory First Year, during which attempts are made to teach people who will never do so in this world to write grammatical prose, and to instill a few basic facts relating to the accepted concerns of Western civilization into minds hitherto untouched in this respect.
— (Dr. Jonathan Hullah, narr.) *The Cunning Man*

Learn [philosophy] as the philosophers learned it — by inward quest. Avoid philosophic systems. Idiots love them because they can all band together and piss in a quill and look down on the unenlightened majority. But nobody can teach you more than somebody else's philosophy. You have to make it your own before it's any good.
— (Hugh McWearie) *The Cunning Man*

The greatest teacher is he who has passed through scorn of mankind, to love of mankind. — (Apollo) *A Masque of Aesop*

Education, if it is real and not a sham, is a releasing, not an imprisoning, thing. — *One Half of Robertson Davies*

Education does not really alter character, but merely intensifies it, making foolish people more foolish, superstitious people more superstitious, and of course wise people wiser. But the wise are few and lonely.
— *The Table Talk of Samuel Marchbanks*

England

There'll always be an England while there is a U.S.A.
— *The Table Talk of Samuel Marchbanks*

Like any good English family, we followed the custom of
the day: convicts to Australia — bastards to Canada.
— *High Spirits*

The British have some odd talents, and writing obituaries
is one of them. — (Simon Darcourt) *What's Bred in the Bone*

Ethnicity

Gypsy blood was not a thing to be proud of — unless one
happened to have it oneself, and knew what Gypsy pride
was like. Not the assertive pride of the boastful Celts and
Teutons and Anglo-Saxons, but something akin to the
pride of the Jews, a sense of being different and special.
— (Maria Theotoky) *The Rebel Angels*

The Welsh and the Scots are the only people who really
understand the fine points of relationship, and I think that
the Welsh have a slight edge on the Scots in this matter.
— *Samuel Marchbanks' Almanack*

Faith / Religion

Faith is a great gift and, atheist as the Professor was in matters of religion, he was not troubled by even the slightest agnosticism concerning himself and his abilities.

— *Leaven of Malice*

It is what is taken for granted in our homes, rather than what we are painstakingly taught, which supplies the bones of our faith. — *A Mixture of Frailties*

Moral judgments belong to God, and it is part of God's mercy that we do not have to undertake that heavy part of His work, even when the judgment concerns ourselves.

— (Sir Benedict Domdaniel) *A Mixture of Frailties*

Do not suppose I was becoming "religious"; the Presbyterianism of my childhood effectively insulated me against any enthusiastic abandonment to faith.

— (Dunstan Ramsay, narr.) *Fifth Business*

Joseph is history's most celebrated cuckold.

— (Padre Blazon) *Fifth Business*

Mankind cannot endure perfection; it stifles him. He demands that even the saints should cast a shadow. If they, these holy ones who have lived so greatly but who still carry their shadows with them, can approach God, well then, there is hope for the worst of us. — (Padre Blazon) *Fifth Business*

Be sure you choose what you believe and know why you believe it, because if you don't choose your beliefs, you may be certain that some belief, and probably not a very creditable one, will choose you.
— (Dunstan Ramsay) *The Manticore*

Christianity enjoins us to seek only the good and to have nothing whatever to do with evil.
— (Dunstan Ramsay) *World of Wonders*

We all interpret Holy Writ to suit ourselves as much as we dare. — (Magnus Eisengrim, narr.) *World of Wonders*

How many visions of Eternity have been born of low blood sugar? — (Simon Darcourt, narr.) *The Rebel Angels*

You're a real Protestant; your prayer is "O God, forgive me, but for God's sake keep this under Your hat."
— (Simon Darcourt, narr.) *The Rebel Angels*

People are said to be drifting away from religion, but few of them drift so far that when they die there is not a call for some kind of religious ceremony. — *The Rebel Angels*

Some of the harsh old theological notions of things are every bit as good, not because they really explain anything, but because at bottom they admit they can't explain a lot of things, so they foist them off on God, who may be cruel and incalculable but at least He takes the guilt for a lot of human misery. – (Simon Darcourt, narr.) *The Rebel Angels*

Without God the skeptic is in a vacuum and his doubt, which is his crowning achievement, is also his tragedy.
– (John Parlabane) *The Rebel Angels*

Isn't the worth of what a man believes shown by what his belief makes of him? – (Maria Theotoky) *The Rebel Angels*

Too much orthodoxy can lead to trouble; a decent measure of come-and-go is more enduring.
– (Simon Darcourt, narr.) *The Rebel Angels*

Adam and Eve left the Garden laughing and happy with their bargain; they had exchanged a know-nothing innocence for infinite choice. – (Arthur Cornish) *The Rebel Angels*

Show me the place in the Bible where it says we are to be happy in this world. Happiness for sinners means sin. You can't get away from it.
– (Victoria Cameron) *What's Bred in the Bone*

Men do not believe in matter today any more than they believe in God; scientists have taught them not to believe in anything. Men of the Middle Ages, and most of them in the Renaissance, believed in God and the things God had made, and they were happier and more complete than we. — (Tancred Saraceni) *What's Bred in the Bone*

The Age of Faith took a deadly disease from the Reformation. Ever see a really great picture inspired by Protestantism? But the passing of the Age of Faith didn't mean the death of art, which is the only immortal, ever-lasting thing. — (Alwyn Ross) *What's Bred in the Bone*

A man who is disposed toward the romantic aspect of religion cannot wholly divorce himself from superstition, though he may pretend to hate it. — *The Lyre of Orpheus*

If God is one and eternal, and if Christ is not dead, but living, are not fashions in art mere follies for those who are the slaves of time? — *The Lyre of Orpheus*

What sort of world have these smashers and destroyers made for me? A world without faith. Or so everybody says. The century past has been a great age of the God-killer. Nietzsche, who was as mad as a hatter, but had some arresting madman's ideas, and without our splendid madmen our culture would be a pretty arid affair. Freud, who asserted

with the persuasive cunning of a powerfully gifted literary man that all faith, all belief, is an illusion, bred of childhood fears. Bertrand Russell, who has no time for faith, but all the time in the world for a variety of Noble Causes, and innocently believes that their nobility resides wholly in their usefulness to mankind. They all want to bring everything down to that – to Man.
– (Conor Gilmartin, narr.) *Murther & Walking Spirits*

Is not Christianity edging close to senility?
– (Conor Gilmartin, narr.) *Murther & Walking Spirits*

Clinical experience has convinced me that God is not particularly interested in examinations, just as he won't be dragged into the Stock Market, or being a backer in show business. – (Dr. Jonathan Hullah, narr.) *The Cunning Man*

A good faith ought to leave lots of leeway.
– (Dr. Jonathan Hullah, narr.) *The Cunning Man*

There's a special kind o' power that comes from the belief that you're right. Whether you really are right or not doesn't matter; it's the belief that counts. – (Pop) *Overlaid*

Revenge is certainly un-Christian but it is not un-human; the Devil is very fond of it, and has coated it in an undeniable sweetness. – *One Half of Robertson Davies*

Our task, if we seek spiritual wholeness, is to be sure that what has been rejected is not, therefore, forgotten, and its possibility wiped out. — *One Half of Robertson Davies*

Saying that God is dead is like saying that there is no Santa Claus; the jolly old man with the white beard may vanish, but the gifts are under the Christmas tree just the same. All that has happened is that the child who thinks it has discovered a great secret no longer feels that it need be good in order to receive gifts; Santa has gone, but parental love is just where it always was. — *One Half of Robertson Davies*

The true realist is he who believes in both God and the Devil, and is prepared to attempt, with humility, to sort out some corner of the extraordinary tangle of their works which is our world. — *A Voice from the Attic*

Is it the final triumph of Protestantism that it has pushed the sacred origin of Christmas so far into the background that most people are able to ignore it?
— *The Diary of Samuel Marchbanks*

Everybody likes to be superstitious about something.
— *Tempest-Tost*

Family

Who really knows his father, or his mother? In our personal dramas they play older, supporting roles, and we are always centre stage, in the limelight.
— (Conor Gilmartin, narr.) *Murther & Walking Spirits*

One's family is made up of supporting players in one's personal drama. One never supposes that they starred in some possibly gaudy and certainly deeply felt show of their own.
— (Hugh McWearie) *Murther & Walking Spirits*

Nobody is so ready to belittle you as your own family.
— (Apollo) *A Masque of Aesop*

Fashions

Nothing grows old-fashioned so fast as modernity.
— *High Spirits*

There are fashions in anxiety and even in degradation.
— *A Voice from the Attic*

Fate

The condition of a vulgarian is that he never expects anything good or bad that happens to him to be the result of his own personality; he always thinks it's Fate, especially if it's bad. The only people who make any sense in the world are those who know that whatever happens to them has its roots in what they are. — (Solomon Bridgetower) *Tempest-Tost*

A man's fate is his own, more than he knows. We attract what we are. — *The Lyre of Orpheus*

If you don't drink your tea while it's hot, you may expect a cold fortune. — (Benoni Richards) *A Jig for the Gypsy*

There is no armour against Fate. — *One Half of Robertson Davies*

Alas, how puny are our best efforts to avert a foreordained event! — *One Half of Robertson Davies*

One must not quarrel with one's fate.
— *The Table Talk of Samuel Marchbanks*

Prophecy consists of carefully bathing the inevitable in the eerie light of the impossible, and then being the first to announce it. — *Samuel Marchbanks' Almanack*

Friendship

Many fine things are written about friendship, and there's a general superstition that everybody is capable of friendship, and gets it, like love. But lots of people never know love, except quite mildly; and most of them never know friendship, except in quite a superficial way. Terribly demanding thing, friendship. Most of us have to put up with acquaintanceship. — (Sir Benedict Domdaniel) *A Mixture of Frailties*

He's an old friend. And we don't always choose our old friends, you know; sometimes we're just landed with them. — (Professor Clement Hollier) *The Rebel Angels*

Genius

Geniuses are not people to make a woman happy. — (Amy Nelson) *A Mixture of Frailties*

He was a genius — that is to say, a man who does superlatively and without obvious effort something that most people cannot do by the uttermost exertion of their abilities. — (Dunstan Ramsay, narr.) *Fifth Business*

Genius is the only true aristocracy.
— (Dr. Gunilla Dahl-Soot) *The Lyre of Orpheus*

Good taste is, after all, a thing that any donkey can learn; the effects of genius are not so easily mastered.
— *Renown at Stratford*

Guilt

A recognition of the guilt in oneself is a necessity to psychological wholeness – not goodness, but wholeness, which is a larger concept. And the ambiguity of guilt – the apparent good deed that brings an evil consequence, and the seeming evil deed that bears good fruit – presents a philosophical problem that few of us are able to meet and vanquish. — *The Mirror of Nature*

Hypocrisy is fertile soil for guilt. — *The Mirror of Nature*

Happiness

Happiness. It is a catlike emotion; if you try to coax it, happiness will avoid you, but if you pay no attention to it, it will

rub against your legs and spring unbidden into your lap.
Forget happiness, and pin your hopes on understanding.
— *One Half of Robertson Davies*

Happiness often gives an effect of shallowness.
— *A Voice from the Attic*

Unhappiness of the kind that is recognized and examined
and brooded over is a spiritual luxury.
— (Magnus Eisengrim, narr.) *World of Wonders*

Health

You can't win in the fight for health.
— *The Table Talk of Samuel Marchbanks*

Health isn't making everybody into a Greek ideal; it's living
out the destiny of the body.
— (Professor Ozias Froats) *The Rebel Angels*

Heroes

Hero worship has value in relation to the hero chosen.
— *A Voice from the Attic*

The modern hero is the man who conquers in the inner struggle. — (Dr. Liselotte Naegeli) *The Manticore*

Hero-worship is important to [men], and when it has passed, it is false to yourself to forget what the hero once meant. — (Professor Clement Hollier) *The Rebel Angels*

Isn't every man who has what it takes to be a Hero terribly alone? — (Arnak) *Question Time*

The gods destroy the heroes with a sudden blow, but they grind us mediocrities for weary, weary years.
— (Dr. Jonathan Hullah, narr.) *The Cunning Man*

Every democratic realist knows that part of the cost of democracy is the gelding of the Hero.
— (The Secretary of State) *Question Time*

Hope

To lose all hope is, in a way, to be free, and it often brings with it a lightening of mood. — *A Mixture of Frailties*

In every immigrant there is hope. Some of them bring nothing but the rags and tatters of the old world. But others bring the shining promise of the world that is to be.
— (Ursula Simonds) *Fortune, My Foe*

The Human Condition

Everybody can share in grief, and grief can be feigned; but laughter can only be shared by those who are of like mind.
— *A Voice from the Attic*

There is a touch of the fascist in most adolescents; they admire the strong man who stands no nonsense; they have no objection to seeing the weak trampled underfoot; mercy in its more subtle forms is outside their understanding and has no meaning for them. — *Tempest-Tost*

The eye sees only what the mind is prepared to comprehend. — *Tempest-Tost*

We always undervalue what we have never been without.
— *Tempest-Tost*

The time for a show of strength is when you're strong.
— (Mr. Snelgrove, Attorney) *Leaven of Malice*

People who mind their own business die of boredom at thirty. — (Humphrey Cobbler) *A Mixture of Frailties*

Some people are born with huge, gusty typhoons of feeling, all ready to be unleashed. Others have to learn to feel. And when they're both forty, you'd have a hard time telling one from the other. But when they're fifty the typhoons will be getting weaker, and the feeling which has been carefully nurtured and schooled may well be growing still.
— (Sir Benedict Domdaniel) *A Mixture of Frailties*

Most people reach a point where they're wishing experience would stop crowding them. Anyhow, it isn't what happens to you that really counts: it's what you are able to do with it. — (Sir Benedict Domdaniel) *A Mixture of Frailties*

It is beautifying to be seen naked by those we love, and the body grows ugly if it is always huddled under clothes. Nakedness is always honesty, and sometimes it is beauty: but even the finest clothes have a hint of vulgarity.
— (Giles Revelstoke) *A Mixture of Frailties*

The young are usually, out of sheer good nature, ready to indulge the sometimes clumsy romantic ideas of their elders. — *A Mixture of Frailties*

Pretense is wonderfully stimulating to the artistic mind, which is why some people lie for fun, rather than from necessity. — *A Mixture of Frailties*

. . . we all think of ourselves as stars and rarely recognize it when we are indeed mere supporting characters or even supernumeraries. — *Fifth Business*

Funerals are among the few ceremonial occasions left to us, and we assume our roles almost without thinking.
— (David Staunton, narr.) *The Manticore*

I know what a heavy burden everybody carries of the unconfessed, which sometimes appears to be the unspeakable. Very often such stuff is not disgraceful or criminal; it is merely a sense of not having behaved well or having done something one knew to be contrary to someone else's good; of having snatched when one should have waited decently; of having turned a sharp corner when someone else was thereby left in a difficult situation; of having talked of the first-rate when one was planning to the second-rate; of having fallen below whatever standards one had set oneself.
— (David Staunton, narr.) *The Manticore*

It is not hard to be popular with any group, whether composed of the most conventional Canadians or of Central
European freaks, if one is prepared to talk to people about
themselves. — (Dunstan Ramsay, narr.) *Fifth Business*

There is no court in the world that can provide a rescript on
past griefs. — (David Staunton, narr.) *The Manticore*

It is a widespread idea that people who are unusually cruel
must be insane, though the corollary of that would be that
anybody who is unusually compassionate must be insane.
— (David Staunton, narr.) *The Manticore*

Everybody needs his mask, and the only intentional impos-
tors are those whose mask is one of a man with nothing to
conceal. We all have much to conceal, and we must conceal
it for our soul's good. — (Dr. J. von Haller) *The Manticore*

Every man who amounts to a damn has several fathers, and
the man who begat him in lust or drink or for a bet or even
in the sweetness of honest love may not be the most important father. The fathers you choose for yourself are the
significant ones. — (Dunstan Ramsay) *The Manticore*

None of us counts for much in the long, voiceless, inert
history of the stone. — (Dunstan Ramsay) *The Manticore*

It's always strangers who turn the tap that lets out the truth.

— (Dr. Liselotte Naegeli) *World of Wonders*

Myth explains much that is otherwise inexplicable, just because myth is a boiling down of universal experience.

— (Dunstan Ramsay) *World of Wonders*

A boy's first recognition of hypocrisy is, or ought to be, more significant than the onset of puberty.

— (Magnus Eisengrim, narr.) *World of Wonders*

Do we not all play, in our minds, with terrible thoughts which we would never dare to put into action? Could we live without some hidden instincts of revolt, of some protest against our fate in life, however enviable it may seem to those who do not have to bear it?

— (Magnus Eisengrim, narr.) *World of Wonders*

How susceptible the young are to embarrassment.

— (Dunstan Ramsay) *World of Wonders*

Egotism, like self-pity, has a bad name, but it is a fact of our existence. With this egotism may very well go a conviction of inner worth, of a fineness which the world does not recognize. — *The Mirror of Nature*

Give no ground to compassion, because the minute you do that a dozen people descend upon you who treat compassion as weakness, and drive you off your course without the slightest regard for what happens to you.
— (Roland Ingestree) *World of Wonders*

Nothing so destroys the sense of equality on which all pleasant social life depends as perpetual reminders that one member of the company outranks all the rest.
— (Dr. Liselotte Naegeli) *World of Wonders*

If it weren't for vanity we should still be running about in our skins, painted a horrid blue. Vanity is one of the mainsprings of human progress. — *High Spirits*

Confidence begets confidence.
— (John Parlabane) *The Rebel Angels*

If you cannot mould yourself as you would wish, how can you expect other people to be entirely to your liking?
— (Simon Darcourt, narr.) *The Rebel Angels*

Silence is entirely a sophisticated, acquired taste. Silence is anti-human. — (John Parlabane) *The Rebel Angels*

One must exaggerate or feel oneself a pygmy.
— (Archey Deloney) *The Rebel Angels*

Human nature inclines toward dissatisfaction . . .
— (Simon Darcourt, narr.) *The Rebel Angels*

Looking like a lout when you aren't one is just as much affectation as being a dandy.
— (Francis's father) *What's Bred in the Bone*

You know about secrets: they grow more and more mysterious, then suddenly they crumple away and everybody wonders why they were ever secret.
— (The Daimon Maimas) *What's Bred in the Bone*

People who live in beautiful surroundings grow accustomed to them, and even indifferent to them. — *The Lyre of Orpheus*

The wax of human experience is always the same. It is we who put our own stamp on it.
— (Simon Darcourt) *The Lyre of Orpheus*

A virtue in excess may slither into a weakness.
— *The Lyre of Orpheus*

One often misses the afflictions and inadequacies of the past as truly as its splendours.
— (ETAH in Limbo) *The Lyre of Orpheus*

How fully does one ever know anybody?
— (Conor Gilmartin, narr.) *Murther & Walking Spirits*

Oh, what a god we have made of the mind, the under-standing, which is so necessary to life, but which hangs like a cloud in the sky above the physical world which is the totality of every human creature! The mind: a trifler! Feeling is more than what happens in the mind; feeling possesses the whole living being.
— (Conor Gilmartin, narr.) *Murther & Walking Spirits*

We all need to take aboard a certain amount of rubbish to keep us all human.
— (Conor Gilmartin, narr.) *Murther & Walking Spirits*

The mind can only endure so much grandeur.
— (Conor Gilmartin, narr.) *Murther & Walking Spirits*

Never harbour grudges; they sour your stomach and do no harm to anyone else. — (Rhodri Cooper) *Murther & Walking Spirits*

Clarity is not a characteristic of the human spirit.
— (Dr. Jonathan Hullah, narr.) *The Cunning Man*

Never neglect the charms of narrative for the human heart.
— (Dunstan Ramsay) *The Cunning Man*

One matures by fits and starts, not by gradual process.
— (Dr. Jonathan Hullah, narr.) *The Cunning Man*

His heart was in the right place — as we so often say of people whose minds are sadly astray.
— (Dr. Jonathan Hullah, narr.) *The Cunning Man*

It's everybody's bounden duty to remember as much as possible about everything that's come under their notice.
— (Esme Barron) *The Cunning Man*

It is so easy to plan lives of humanitarian self-sacrifice for other people. — (Dr. Jonathan Hullah, narr.) *The Cunning Man*

We're all pitiable, one way or another. You must submit to being pitied, just like everybody else.
— (Brochwel Gilmartin) *The Cunning Man*

We minor actors must "play as cast" and be glad of the work. — (Dr. Jonathan Hullah, narr.) *The Cunning Man*

It takes two to make charm.
— (Dr. Maria Clementina Sobieska) *Hunting Stuart*

Fail, and the world fails with you; succeed and you succeed alone. — (Nicholas Hayward) *Fortune, My Foe*

That is the tragedy of age; no one ever really feels old.
— (Professor Idris Rowlands) *Fortune, My Foe*

The more thoroughly and committedly you become a professional person, the greater is the danger that you will cease to be a private person. That is where the danger lies. One of the serious troubles with our modern world is that far too many people have become so identified with their public life and their public role that they have lost sight of the private person that they must also be. The public figure is a giant: the private person is a dwarf. — *One Half of Robertson Davies*

Don't be surprised if you find that nobody wants you except in your professional capacity. — *One Half of Robertson Davies*

Pride is, among other things, egotism.
— *One Half of Robertson Davies*

The world is full of people whose notion of a satisfactory future is, in fact, a return to an idealized past.
— *A Voice from the Attic*

Some illnesses are necessary and salutary, and indeed should not be called sicknesses but processes of evolution.
— *The Mirror of Nature*

Upon the pleasures of the past the sun never sets, and over its horrors the iniquity of oblivion blindly scattereth her poppy. — *The Diary of Samuel Marchbanks*

The points of resemblance between great people and paltry people are infinitely more numerous than the points of difference: they all eat, sleep, fall in love, catch cold, and use handkerchiefs. — *The Table Talk of Samuel Marchbanks*

A wildly rolling eye is invariably the accompaniment of a proud and daring spirit. — *The Table Talk of Samuel Marchbanks*

Human beings are that and nothing more, and . . . it is unreasonable to expect them to behave like angels. It is unreasonable to expect the uneducated to behave like the educated; it is unreasonable to expect the ethical to behave like the unethical; it is unreasonable to expect the hungry to behave like the replete, the poor like the rich, and the unhappy like the happy. We must not find fault with people because they often fall short of perfect virtue. We may hope for the best, but we should not be unduly downcast when it does not come to pass. A great part of the world's misery is the result of this foolish expectation that people are always going to be on their best behaviour. Man is born sinful; the remarkable thing is not that man fails to be wholly good, but that he is as good as he is.
— *Samuel Marchbanks' Almanack*

Always in history there are those who are impelled, by reasons they think sufficient, to ruin, insofar as they can, what the patient, indefatigable warriors of civilization and culture have built up, because they value other things and worship other gods.
— (Conor Gilmartin, narr.) *Murther & Walking Spirits*

The only equality we have is our common humanity.
— (The Minister for External Affairs) *Question Time*

It is the manifest duty of humble people to stop being humble just as fast as they can, because the shadow of their humility is a know-nothing, cantankerous self-righteousness.
— *One Half of Robertson Davies*

Humour

Wit is something you possess, but humour is something that possesses you.
— (Professor Clement Hollier) *The Rebel Angels*

A sense of humour, like every good gift, has a positive and a negative side.
— (Conor Gilmartin, narr.) *Murther & Walking Spirits*

When educated people joke, it is a good idea to look at the underside of the joke; there may be a significant truth under there which less educated people could not cloak in a jest. – (Dr. Jonathan Hullah, narr.) *The Cunning Man*

Never be deceived by a humorist, for if he is any good he is a deeply serious man, moved by a quirk of temperament to speak a certain kind of truth in the form of jokes. Everybody can laugh at the jokes; the real trick is to understand them. – *One Half of Robertson Davies*

A great sense of humour can only exist in company with other elements of greatness. – *A Voice from the Attic*

Humour is a civilizing element in the jungle of the mind, and civilizing elements never enjoy a complete or prolonged popularity. – *A Voice from the Attic*

Don't you know what humour is? Universities redefine wit and satire every few years; surely it is time they nailed down humour for us? I don't know what it is, though I suspect that it is an attribute of everything, and the substance of nothing, so if I had to define a sense of humour I would say it lay in the perception of shadows.
– *Samuel Marchbanks' Almanack*

Insults

Not all the Irish are idiots; they have a lot of Spanish blood, you know. – (Padre Blazon) *Fifth Business*

. . . a mind like a morgue in which a variety of defunct ideas lay on slabs, kept cold to defer decay.
– (David Staunton, narr.) *The Manticore*

Fat Ladies ought not to tell jokes; their mirth is of the flesh, not of the mind. – (Magnus Eisengrim, narr.) *World of Wonders*

His square, granite face was marked with the look of intense disapproval so often seen in the Scot who has risen high in the world. – *High Spirits*

A powerful conscience and no sense of humour – a dangerous combination. – (Simon Darcourt, narr.) *The Rebel Angels*

His breath suggested that he was dying from within, and had completed about two-thirds of the job.
– *What's Bred in the Bone*

[He] . . . was on the whole good-natured and untroubled by intelligence. – *What's Bred in the Bone*

He was a man whose enthusiasms sometimes outran his judgment. — *What's Bred in the Bone*

Even the blind pig sometimes finds an acorn.
— (Geraint Powell) *The Lyre of Orpheus*

I know that I am at anchor in the stream of progress . . .
— *The Diary of Samuel Marchbanks*

The Apotheosis of the Yahoo is one of the primary objects of Hollywood. — *The Diary of Samuel Marchbanks*

My dullness is so complete and all-embracing that it constitutes a kind of mystical experience — the merging of the Null with the Void. — *The Table Talk of Samuel Marchbanks*

I detest Turkish sweets. They appear to me to be made of raw mutton fat into which low-caste Turks have ground caraway seeds by rubbing it between the soles of their feet.
— *Samuel Marchbanks' Almanack*

Posture is a word I prefer not to use in connection with myself. — *Samuel Marchbanks' Almanack*

Intellect

What a cruel joker and mean master the intellect can be.
— (Dunstan Ramsay, narr.) *Fifth Business*

It is a terrible thing for an intellectual when he encounters an idea as a reality. — (Simon Darcourt, narr.) *The Rebel Angels*

The day has gone when people feel that they can be unashamedly arrogant about superior intellect.
— (Professor Clement Hollier) *The Rebel Angels*

The aristocracy of intellect admits nothing of democracy.
— (Conor Gilmartin, narr.) *Murther & Walking Spirits*

There is no democracy in the world of intellect.
— *A Voice from the Attic*

If we seek to encompass all that we can of the spectrum of human intellect and feeling, we cannot confine ourselves to the reds and oranges; we must know the violets and indigos as well. — *A Voice from the Attic*

A few hundred quiet intellectuals do not make an awakened country; only an aware, alert, tirelessly curious middle class can do that. — *One Half of Robertson Davies*

Journalism

If you want the benefit of what journalists do, you must put up with some of the annoyance of what they do, as well.
— (Gloster Ridley) *Leaven of Malice*

Persons seeking to enter the profession of journalism are usually sodden with romantic notions about it, and particularly about the big rewards it brings. Marchbanks' Journalistic Training Course was simple: "(a) Read all of the Bible, or at least three-quarters of it, because it is a classical education, a history, and a compendium of ancient wisdom; (b) read the Book of Common Prayer, as a lesson in style, and also of good manners toward your superiors (a grave lack among journalists as a class); (c) read the *Complete Works of Shakespeare*, for knowledge of human nature and vocabulary; (d) read Defoe's *Robinson Crusoe* until you have mastered his ability to make dubious, and even imaginary things seem true. Do not bleat about 'the public's right to know' when you really mean your own right to snoop. But snoop, all the same, and keep your trap shut about your sources or they will turn on you and destroy you." — *The Table Talk of Samuel Marchbanks*

Editors at best are disagreeable fellows, professional contradicters and sassers back. — *The Table Talk of Samuel Marchbanks*

There is a widespread delusion that newspaper-men always know the news. — (Edward Weir) *Fortune, My Foe*

Language

Funny how languages break down and turn into something else. Latin was rubbed away until it degenerated into dreadful lingos like French and Spanish and Italian, and lo! people found out that quite new things could be said in these degenerate tongues – things nobody had ever thought of in Latin. — (Simon Darcourt, narr.) *The Rebel Angels*

I would rather listen to somebody who loved meanings better than words themselves, a speaker who would remain silent rather than use a word he did not truly know. — *One Half of Robertson Davies*

Without precision of meaning we damage not simply language, but thought. — *One Half of Robertson Davies*

Latin and Greek, if they teach us anything, teach us compression, and compression is a form of elegance. — *One Half of Robertson Davies*

Lawyers

Patience must be the watchword of the successful litigant.
— *Samuel Marchbanks' Almanack*

A lawyer who dies without a will is one of the jokes of the profession. — (David Staunton, narr.) *The Manticore*

Many lawyers are beetle-witted ignoramuses, prey to their own emotions and those of their clients; some of them work up big practices because they can fling themselves fiercely into other people's fights. Their indignation is for sale. — (David Staunton, narr.) *The Manticore*

Life

One of the really notable achievements of the twentieth century has been to make the young old before their time.
— (Solomon Bridgetower) *Tempest-Tost*

Most hearts of any quality are broken on two or three occasions in a lifetime. They mend, of course, and are often stronger than before, but something of the essence of life is lost at every break. — *Leaven of Malice*

You think life has trapped you, do you? Well, my friend, everybody is trapped, more or less. The best thing you can hope for is to understand your trap and make terms with it, tooth by tooth. — (Humphrey Cobbler) *Leaven of Malice*

I think one of the secrets of life is that one must give up caring too much about anything. I know that sounds terrible, but for a lot of people it's the only possible philosophy. You blunt the edge of fate by being stoical.
— (Solomon Bridgetower) *A Mixture of Frailties*

I have never thought that traits that are strong in childhood disappear; they may go underground or they may be transmuted into something else, but they do not vanish; very often they make a vigorous appearance after the meridian of life has been passed. It is this, and not senility, that is the real second childhood. — (Dunstan Ramsay, narr.) *Fifth Business*

As we neared our sixties the cloaks we wrapped about our essential selves were wearing thin.
— (Dunstan Ramsay, narr.) *Fifth Business*

Charity is the last lesson we learn. That is why so much of the charity we show people is retrospective.
— (Dr. J. von Haller) *The Manticore*

I suppose unless you are unlucky, anywhere you spend your summers as a child is an Arcadia forever.

— (David Staunton, narr.) *The Manticore*

To be cynical is not the same as avoiding illusion, for cynicism is just another kind of illusion. All formulas for meeting life – even many philosophies – are illusion.

— (Boy Staunton) *The Manticore*

These mysterious ailments that take us out of life but do not kill us. They are signals that our life is going the wrong way, and intervals for reflection. — (Dr. J. von Haller) *The Manticore*

Almost everything of great value I have learned in life has been taught me by women.

— (Magnus Eisengrim, narr.) *World of Wonders*

Everybody's life is his Passion.

— (Dr. Liselotte Naegeli) *World of Wonders*

Part of the glory and terror of our life is that somehow, at some time, we get all that's coming to us. Everybody gets their lumps and their bouquets and it goes on for quite a while after death. — (Magnus Eisengrim, narr.) *World of Wonders*

Without some measure of illusion life becomes intolerable.

— (Maria Theotoky) *The Rebel Angels*

Life must be lived, and sometimes living means enduring.
— *What's Bred in the Bone*

Better to suffer and live, and taste the full bitterness of suffering, than to hop the twig.
— (Conor Gilmartin, narr.) *Murther & Walking Spirits*

Suicide, for all its horror, is, in the last consideration, a frivolity, an attempt to be an exception in the proper order of life. Jumping the queue, so to speak.
— *Murther & Walking Spirits*

The more rough-and-tumble you experience early in life, the better armed you are against what's to follow.
— (Brochwel Gilmartin) *The Cunning Man*

This is the Great Theatre of Life. Admission is free but the taxation is mortal. You come when you can, and leave when you must. The show is continuous. Good night.
— *The Cunning Man*

The outward trappings of life are not the innermost secrets of life. — Introduction to *At My Heart's Core*

The good life is lived not widely, but deeply. It is not doing things, but understanding what you do that brings real excitement and lasting pleasure. — *One Half of Robertson Davies*

Live shallowly, and you will find yourself surrounded by shallow people. — *One Half of Robertson Davies*

Failure at a specific task is always disagreeable and sometimes it is humiliating. But there is only one kind of failure that really breaks the spirit, and that is failure in the art of life itself. That is the failure that one does well to fear.
— *One Half of Robertson Davies*

What will make him an old man is a frightened clinging to the values of the first half of life. We have all seen these juvenile dotards whose boast is that they are just as young as their sons or their grandsons; they do not realize what a pitiful boast that is. They prate about their sympathy with youth, but they mean only the superficialities and ephemera of youth. Many of the sad smashups in marriages that we all see among middle-aged people have their origin in this attempt to dodge an inescapable fact. The values that are proper and all-absorbing during the first half of life will not sustain a man during the second half. If he has the courage and wisdom to advance courageously into the new realm of values and emotions he will age physically, of course, but his intellectual and spiritual growth will continue, and will give satisfaction to himself and to all those associated with him. And such courage and wisdom are by no means rare; they may show themselves among many people who have never thought along these lines at all but who have a knack for living life wisely; and they also are to be found among those who regard self-awareness as one of the primary duties of a good life. Paradoxically, such people are on better terms with youth than the shrivelled Peter Pans who dare not be their age. — *One Half of Robertson Davies*

Myth and fairy tales are nothing less than the distilled truth about what we call "real life," and that we move through a throng of Sleeping Princesses, Belle Dames sans Merci, Cinderellas, Wicked Witches, Powerful Wizards, Frog Princes, Lucky Third Sons, Ogres, Dwarves, Sagacious Animal Helpers and Servers, yes and Heroes and Heroines, in a world that is nothing less than an enchanted landscape, and that life only seems dull and spiritless to those who live under a spell — too often a spell they have brought upon their own heads. — *One Half of Robertson Davies*

Gross insanity among the poor and unfortunate becomes neurosis, or oddity, or eccentricity among those who are more fortunately placed in society. — *One Half of Robertson Davies*

The "unlived" life . . . : It is very often the life that has been put aside in order to serve the demands of a career, or an idea of one's place in the world, or simply to serve one's own comfort and egotism. Very often it is love that is sacrificed in this way, but it may also be adventure, or a concern with the arts, or friendship, or simply a greater freedom of action: these unlived elements revenge themselves and sometimes they do it with compounded interest.

— *One Half of Robertson Davies*

Let the philosophers and the physicists say what they will, time for most of us is the fleeting instant we call Now. Any enjoyment or profit we get from life, we get Now; to kill Now is to abridge our own lives. — *A Voice from the Attic*

Not ends, but means must be the concern of those who seek satisfaction in the pleasures as well as the obligations of life. — *A Voice from the Attic*

To experience deep feeling only in the fashionable modes of our time is to limit ourselves foolishly and to ensure that as the years pass, we shall ourselves become back numbers — for nothing changes so quickly as mere fashion.

— *A Voice from the Attic*

The fantasy life is not an end in itself, but a long road by which we travel toward the deepest truth about ourselves; to close that road is to deny much of the best life has to give.

— *A Voice from the Attic*

The life of Man is a struggle with Nature and a struggle with the Machine; when Nature and the Machine link forces against him, Man hasn't a chance.
— *The Diary of Samuel Marchbanks*

If we were all robbed of our wrong convictions, how empty our lives would be. — *The Diary of Samuel Marchbanks*

The really deep things of life are impervious to satire.
— *Samuel Marchbanks' Almanack*

Literature

If we must have apparitions, by all means let them be literate. — *High Spirits*

Literature is an essence, not a piquant sauce.
— (Conor Gilmartin, narr.) *Murther & Walking Spirits*

Criticism is comparatively easy in its showy but superficial aspect. Anybody can pick up its techniques and use them with a display of skill, just as anybody can make a spectacular cut with a surgeon's scalpel, simply because it is so sharp. But the vastly more difficult business of discovering literature, and giving oneself wholly into its embrace, and making some of it part of oneself, cannot be done in large classes, and not everybody can do it even in small classes. A surprising number of people can get Ph.D.'s in criticism; to be a worthy reader of what writers of conscience have written is a very different matter. — *One Half of Robertson Davies*

Literature of the first order does not deal with types, but with individuals. — *One Half of Robertson Davies*

The Christian urge for nearly two thousand years has been toward a perfection that we profess to admire; but when we are off guard, it is wholeness rather than perfection that we are interested in and the full development of human possibility is what we ask of literature. — *One Half of Robertson Davies*

It is by putting Man in the highest position in the universe that we diminish the vigour and tension of literary art. — *One Half of Robertson Davies*

Not to be acquainted with what is happening in literary France is to feel disgraced, and in the pecking order of literary criticism a Frenchman can humiliate an Englishman just as readily as an Englishman can humiliate an American, and an American a Canadian. One of Canada's most serious literary needs at present is some lesser nation to domineer over and shame by displays of superior taste. — *A Voice from the Attic*

It is axiomatic that if a thing is supposed to be true, it can be immeasurable more lurid and crude than if it is labelled as fiction. — *A Voice from the Attic*

Love

No man should ever assume that he will be able to get the immediate and undivided attention of a woman who has children. — *Leaven of Malice*

Love and a cough cannot be hid.
— (David Staunton, narr.) *The Manticore*

Most men, when they fall in love, hang some sort of label on the woman they want, and attribute to her all sorts of characteristics that are not really hers.
— (Maria Theotoky) *The Rebel Angels*

Nobody gets through life without a broken heart.
— (The Daimon Maimas) *What's Bred in the Bone*

A heart is never really stout until it has broken and mended at least once. — (The Daimon Maimas) *What's Bred in the Bone*

We all have our early loves whom we keep in the back of our minds all our lives. — (Princess Amalie) *The Lyre of Orpheus*

Flirtation's a good old sport and due for a revival.
— (Geraint Powell) *The Lyre of Orpheus*

That's one of the big mistakes, you know — that everybody loves in the same way and that everybody may have a great love. You might as well say that everybody can compose a great symphony. A lot of love is misery; bad weather punctuated by occasional flashes of sunlight.
— (Geraint Powell) *The Lyre of Orpheus*

What does anybody ever see in someone else's love affairs?
— (Conor Gilmartin, narr.) *Murther & Walking Spirits*

Romance can't be laid on the table and carved up like a cadaver, to see what once made it live.
— (Conor Gilmartin, narr.) *Murther & Walking Spirits*

Flattery is the real expert's technique of seduction. Beats knee-squeezing forty different ways.
— (Dr. Jonathan Hullah, narr.) *The Cunning Man*

Every old man ought to have a regretted lost love.
— (Dr. Jonathan Hullah, narr.) *The Cunning Man*

Longing is some of the best of loving.
— (Dr. Jonathan Hullah, narr.) *The Cunning Man*

Every love affair is a private madness into which nobody else can hope to penetrate. — (Hugh McWearie) *The Cunning Man*

Love lays heavy burdens on the loved one, sometimes.
— *The Cunning Man*

When a young man is about to fall in love, one of the earliest symptoms is a keen dissatisfaction with his mother.
— (Aristophontes) *Eros at Breakfast*

Is there a man anywhere who is capable of filling the whole of a woman's heart forever?
— (The Hon. Thomas Stewart) *At My Heart's Core*

The formality and the pattern, either in love or in entertaining, is half the fun. — *One Half of Robertson Davies*

Love, like ice cream, is a beautiful thing, but nobody should regard it as adequate provision for a long and adventurous journey. — *The Diary of Samuel Marchbanks*

Modern love, as reflected in Valentines, is on a depressingly infantile level. — *The Table Talk of Samuel Marchbanks*

Loyalty

Be discreet in your loyalties, or your dwelling will not only be the home of lost causes, but the refuge of impossible people. — *Samuel Marchbanks' Almanack*

Those who parade their loyalty hope to gain by it.
— (Henry Benedict Stuart) *Hunting Stuart*

Luck

Intellectual endowment is a factor in a man's fate, and so is character, and so is industry, and so is courage, but they can all go right down the drain without another factor that nobody likes to admit, and that's sheer, bald-headed Luck.
— (Simon Darcourt, narr.) *The Rebel Angels*

A light heart, or a consciousness of desert, attracts ill luck.
— (Solomon Bridgetower) *Tempest-Tost*

We all bring ill-luck to others, often without in the least recognizing it. — (Padre Blazon) *Fifth Business*

We are all dealt a hand of cards at birth; if somebody gets a rotten hand, full of twos and threes and nothing above a five, what chance has he against the fellow with a full flush? — (Arthur Cornish) *What's Bred in the Bone*

Of course everybody is dealt a hand, but now and then he has a chance to draw another card, and it's the card he draws when the chance comes that can make all the difference. — (Simon Darcourt) *What's Bred in the Bone*

What happens to people is so often nothing but the luck of the game. — (Arthur Cornish) *What's Bred in the Bone*

Mankind

People don't by any means all live in what we call the present; the psychic structure of modern man lurches and yaws over a span of at least ten thousand years.
— (Professor Clement Hollier) *The Rebel Angels*

About the virtues of baptism he had no doubt. Its solely Christian implications apart, it was the acceptance of a new life into a society that thereby declared that it had a place for that new life; it was an assertion of an attitude toward life that was expressed in the Creed which was a part of the service in a form archaic and compressed but full of noble implication. The parents and godparents might think they did not believe that Creed, as they recited it, but it was plain that they were living in a society which had its roots in that Creed; if there had been no Creed, and no cause for formulation of that Creed, vast portions of civilization would never have come into being, and those who smiled at the Creed or disregarded it altogether nevertheless stood firmly on its foundation. The Creed was one of the great signposts in the journey of mankind from a primitive society toward whatever was to come, and though the signpost might be falling behind in the march of civilization, it had marked a great advance from which there could be no permanent retreat. — *The Lyre of Orpheus*

If you're too fine for the funnies, you're too fine for life. They show you what the people are thinking who never read a book, never hear a sermon, and forget to vote. Does that make them worthless? Not on your life. The funnies give you the dreams and opinions of *l'homme moyen sensuel*, and if you want to be a politician, for instance, that's the place to start. Understand the funnies, and you've made a good beginning on understanding mankind.
— (Brochwel Gilmartin) *The Cunning Man*

It is paradoxical that the more often mankind gets into hot water, the better off it is.
— (Dr. Jonathan Hullah, narr.) *The Cunning Man*

Mankind, it appears to me, seeks gloves with which to clothe the iron hand of Necessity, and these gloves he calls diseases. – (Dr. Jonathan Hullah, narr.) *The Cunning Man*

To be a creator is to be in touch, sometimes in uncomfortably close touch, with what psychiatrists call the Unconscious – and not always one's personal Unconscious, but the vast, troubled Unconscious of mankind.
– *One Half of Robertson Davies*

Ritual is man's way of evoking what is too great for realistic portrayal. – *Renown at Stratford*

It is trivial to say that power, or even vice, are more interesting than virtue, and people say so only when they have not troubled to take a look at virtue and see how amazing, and sometimes inhuman and unlikable, it really is.
– (David Staunton, narr.) *The Manticore*

If a man wants to be the greatest possible value to his fellow creatures let him begin the long solitary task of perfecting himself. – (Richard Roberts) *A Jig for the Gypsy*

Manners

We live in the age of the sweatshirt and the jeans. Charm and manners are out. But they'll come back. They always do. Look at the French Revolution: in a generation or two the French were all hopping around like fleas, bowing and scraping to Napoleon. People love manners, really. They admit you to one or another of a dozen secret societies.
— (Arthur Cornish) *The Lyre of Orpheus*

Marriage

No girl thinks very much about marrying a man seriously older than herself. — *A Mixture of Frailties*

Never marry your childhood sweetheart; the reasons that make you choose her will all turn into reasons why you should have rejected her. — (Boy Staunton) *The Manticore*

A deceived husband is merely a cuckold, a figure of fun, whereas a deceived wife is someone who has sustained an injury. — (David Staunton, narr.) *The Manticore*

Cuckolds are fated to play ignominious and usually comic roles. — *What's Bred in the Bone*

No wise man marries a woman if he can't stand her mother.
— (Simon Darcourt) *The Lyre of Orpheus*

The marriages that worked best were those in which the unity still permitted of some separateness — not a ranting independence, but a firm possession by both man and woman of their own souls. — *The Lyre of Orpheus*

Marriage isn't just domesticity, or the continuance of the race, or institutionalized sex, or a form of property right. And it damned well isn't happiness, as that word is generally used. I think it's a way of finding your soul.
— (Simon Darcourt) *The Lyre of Orpheus*

Every marriage involves not two, but four people. There are the two that are seen before the altar, or the city clerk, or whoever links them, but they are attended invisibly by two others, and those invisible ones may prove very soon to be of equal or even greater importance. There is the Woman who is concealed in the Man, and there is the Man who is concealed in the Woman. That's the marriage quaternity, and anybody who fails to understand it must be very simple, or bound for trouble. — (Hugh McWearie) *Murther & Walking Spirits*

An affair is far harder to maintain over a long period than a marriage. In a marriage the friend may gradually and without trouble alternate with or take precedence over the

lover, but in an affair there must always be a pretense that heat of passion is still what keeps the thing going.
— (Dr. Jonathan Hullah, narr.) *The Cunning Man*

When you marry somebody, you marry his parents, and his aunts and uncles, and a whole tribe of people, some of whom you may never see. But they're all there, just the same. — (Lillian Stuart) *Hunting Stuart*

There is more to marriage than four bare legs in a blanket.
— (Benoni Richards) *A Jig for the Gypsy*

As a general thing, people marry most happily with their own kind. The trouble lies in the fact that people usually marry at an age where they do not really know what their own kind is. — *A Voice from the Attic*

It is so easy to pick wives for rich young men.
— *Renown at Stratford*

Men

A boy is a man in miniature, and though he may sometimes exhibit notable virtue, as well as characteristics that seem to be charming because they are childlike, he is also a schemer, self-seeker, traitor, Judas, crook, and villain – in short, a man. – (Dunstan Ramsay, narr.) *Fifth Business*

Most men, without being conscious of the fact, spend a great deal of time and effort in bringing about circumstances which will enable them to support an ideal portrait of themselves which they have created. – *Tempest-Tost*

There are times when every woman is disgusted by the bonelessness of men. – *Tempest-Tost*

There is a point in a man's undressing when he looks stupid, and nothing in the world can make him into a romantic figure. It is at the moment when he stands in his underwear and socks. – *The Manticore*

Most men, unless they are assembled on the lowest, turnip-like principle, have a spell of chivalry at sometime in their lives. – (Dunstan Ramsay) *World of Wonders*

Most men are much more partial to their grandfathers than to their fathers, just as they admire their grandsons but rarely their sons. – (Magnus Eisengrim, narr.) *World of Wonders*

Men always want to disconcert women and put them at a disadvantage . . . – (Maria Theotoky) *The Rebel Angels*

Men who truly don't like flowers are very uncommon and men who don't respond to a beautiful woman are even more uncommon. It's not primarily sexual; it's a lifting of the spirits beauty gives.
— (Professor Clement Hollier) *The Rebel Angels*

Every man likes to think he knows more about women than his father. — *What's Bred in the Bone*

Every man is a king at some time. And if nobody will acknowledge it, he dies — whether he cuts his throat or by a long, slow withering through the years. It is supremely important to secure and cherish the moment of kingship.
— (Dr. Homer Shrubsole) *Hunting Stuart*

Men like girls with jobs; it seems to give them a sense of security. — (Vanessa Medway) *Fortune, My Foe*

When you want to know what a man is, imagine the exact opposite of what he seems; that'll give you the key of his character. — (James "Chilly Jim" Steel) *Fortune, My Foe*

Men mustn't complain about the way women treat them; it makes them look foolish. — (Vanessa Medway) *Fortune, My Foe*

Men who terrify the world are often wretched to look at.
— (Apollo) *A Masque of Aesop*

A man who isn't a hero to his own intelligence is in a pretty bad way. — (Arnak) *Question Time*

A man possessed is a poor commentator on his possession.
— *One Half of Robertson Davies*

Every man needs a study. Not to study in, of course, but to retire to when the pressure of domestic life is too great.
— *One Half of Robertson Davies*

There are two kinds of cigar smokers – patrician fellows, who look as though they had been born to smoke the finest Havana, and people like myself, who look like cannibals gnawing a finger from their latest victim. If one does not belong to the very small first class, one should smoke cigars in private; nothing makes a man look so degraded as a drool-soaked, tattered, burning stump of tobacco stuck in one corner of his mouth. — *Samuel Marchbanks' Almanack*

There is a misanthrope in every man, and the cold germ usually brings him well to the fore . . .
— *The Diary of Samuel Marchbanks*

Does any man like to be told that he is a given point which beginners in his trade soon hope to pass?
— *The Table Talk of Samuel Marchbanks*

Men can be led but they won't be driven; mice, of course, do what they are told. — *The Table Talk of Samuel Marchbanks*

There is a certain spiritual indecency in overhearing any man talking baby talk or making love, but that does not mean that it is wrong or indecent of him to do so.
— *The Table Talk of Samuel Marchbanks*

I do not hold with pretending that our exceptional and great men are made in our image. We honour and follow them for the very reason that they are not.
— *Samuel Marchbanks' Almanack*

The mental age of a man might be gauged by observing how often he can laugh at the same joke.
— *Samuel Marchbanks' Almanack*

Men like children, but they do not like them to be too close. Some barrier — as for instance a wide street, filled with traffic — between a man and a baby, acts as a powerful stimulant to affection between them.
— *Samuel Marchbanks' Almanack*

It does a man good to take a few pills every day. It gives him a feeling that he is taking care of himself, and this persuades him that he is in good health — but only just. It is not advisable to feel too well. People who boast about their good health are apt to overtax it. They want to lift things which should be left on the ground; they insist upon walking when it would be much simpler to ride. Everybody should have some slight, not too obtrusive ailment, which he coddles. Nobody should be without some harmless medicine which he takes. These things enable him to husband his strength, harbour his resources, and live to a ripe old age. — *Samuel Marchbanks' Almanack*

It is men's work, rather than their recreations, which create trouble. — *Samuel Marchbanks' Almanack*

I never know what people mean by "distinguished" when they apply it to a man's appearance. Often the person so described looks as though he smelt a bad drain, or had a nail in his shoe, or had been to the barber and got his hair down his neck; the alliance between distinction and an appearance of suffering appears to be unbreakable. Nobody who looks as though he enjoyed life is ever called distinguished, though he is a man in a million. For some reason the world has decided that an expression suggestive of pain and disgust is a mark of superior mental power, for the world assumes, quite wrongly, that to be happy is a simple thing, within the reach of any idiot. — *The Table Talk of Samuel Marchbanks*

East is East, and West is West, but bachelors are wistful rascals the world over. — *Samuel Marchbanks' Almanack*

It is a favourite notion of romantic young men that misery can be forgotten in work. If the work can be done late at night, all the better. And if the combination of misery and work can be brought together in an attic a very high degree of melancholy self-satisfaction may be achieved, for in spite of the supposed anti-romantic bias of our age the tradition of work, love, attics, drink, and darkness is still powerful. The only real difficulty lies in balancing the level of work against the level of the misery; at any moment the misery is likely to slap over the work, and drown it. — *Tempest-Tost*

Men and Women

Gatherings at which only one sex is represented are rarely enlivening. The only thing drearier than a pack of men eating together is a pack of women doing the same. . . . The sexes are only tolerable when mingled.
— *The Table Talk of Samuel Marchbanks*

An audience entirely of men is bad enough, but an audience entirely of women is as frightening as a battery of machine guns. — *Samuel Marchbanks' Almanack*

After forty-five the differences which divide men from women are trivial compared with those which separate the wise from the unwise, the whole from the fragmented, the survivors from the fallen. — *Samuel Marchbanks' Almanack*

It may be said that in any age men and women of exceptional qualities may be anything they choose, if they have the power of personality or intellect, or spirit, to get away with it. — *The Mirror of Nature*

Every man and woman is a mystery, built like those Chinese puzzles which consist of one box inside another, so that ten or twelve boxes have to be opened before the final solution is found. Not more than two or three people have ever penetrated beyond my outside box, and there are not many people who I have explored further; if anyone imagines that being on first-name terms with somebody magically strips away all the boxes and reveals the inner treasure he still has a great deal to learn about human nature. There are people, of course, who consist only of one box, and that a cardboard carton, containing nothing at all.
— *The Diary of Samuel Marchbanks*

Mind / Body

Beneath what the mind chooses to admit to itself lie convictions that shape our lives. — *What's Bred in the Bone*

Nothing is so easy to fake as the inner vision.
— (President of the Union House Committee) *What's Bred in the Bone*

Of course the mind influences the body; but the body influences the mind, as well, and to take only one side in the argument is to miss much that is — in the true sense of the word — vital. — (Dr. Jonathan Hullah, narr.) *The Cunning Man*

The inert mind is a greater danger than the inert body, for it overlays and stifles the desire to live.
— (Dr. Jonathan Hullah) *The Cunning Man*

Miscellany

Bustle without fatigue: that is the essence of bureaucracy.
— (Chremes) *Eros at Breakfast*

Compassion dulls the mind faster than brandy.
— (Dunstan Ramsay, narr.) *Fifth Business*

Behind every symbol there is a reality.
— (John Scott Ripon) *A Mixture of Frailties*

Paris in Spring is not an easy place in which to nurse a grudge against oneself. — *A Mixture of Frailties*

The dog is a Yes-animal, very popular with people who can't afford to keep a Yes-man. — *The Table Talk of Samuel Marchbanks*

If only things and feelings existed, and thoughts and judgments did not have to trouble and torture!
— (Monica Gall, narr.) *A Mixture of Frailties*

Whose esteem is sweeter than that of an expert in one's own line? — (Dunstan Ramsay, narr.) *Fifth Business*

The free-ranging creature is not always the best of the breed. — (David Staunton, narr.) *The Manticore*

Imagination is a good horse to carry you over the ground, not a flying carpet to set you free from probability.
— (Pargetter) *The Manticore*

In my experience tact is usually worse than the brutalities of truth. — (Roland Ingestree) *World of Wonders*

Life has made me aware of how far mean minds rely on generosity in others. — (Magnus Eisengrim, narr.) *World of Wonders*

Too much cleanliness is an enemy to creation, to speculative thought. — (John Parlabane) *The Rebel Angels*

Simple people demand simple proofs of things that aren't at all simple. — (Simon Darcourt, narr.) *The Rebel Angels*

All authority is capricious, but may be appeased by a show of zeal, unaccompanied by any real work.
— *What's Bred in the Bone*

Monasteries don't send out dogs after escapees.
— (John Parlabane) *The Rebel Angels*

Figures of authority should be composed when they arrive at the scene of whatever human mess awaits them.
— (Simon Darcourt, narr.) *The Rebel Angels*

Even a buzzard sometimes gags.
— (John Parlabane) *The Rebel Angels*

Don't expect me to make an omelette without breaking eggs. — (The Daimon Maimas) *What's Bred in the Bone*

A good long illness can be a blessing.
— (The Daimon Maimas) *What's Bred in the Bone*

Those who find a Master should yield to the Master until they have outgrown him.
— (The Daimon Maimas) *What's Bred in the Bone*

Stinginess does nothing to improve the looks.
— *What's Bred in the Bone*

There's a lot to be said for knowing one's place.
— (Ruth Nibsmith) *What's Bred in the Bone*

Everybody ought to have some experience of being a servant; it is useful to know what virtually unlimited authority is like for those on the receiving end.
— *What's Bred in the Bone*

I know when a pretense of simplicity is a clever play for power. — (Simon Darcourt) *The Lyre of Orpheus*

Those of us who lack the gift of the gab are suspicious of those who have it. — *The Lyre of Orpheus*

Nothing like a good reputation when you are about to commit a crime. — *The Lyre of Orpheus*

There is something about a cupboard that makes a skeleton very restless. — (Simon Darcourt) *The Lyre of Orpheus*

To be ruled by a comic fate is not to feel oneself as a figure of comedy. — (ETAH in Limbo) *The Lyre of Orpheus*

Needs must when the Devil drives.
— (Conor Gilmartin, narr.) *Murther & Walking Spirits*

Surely what knows no bounds must be Eternity.
— (Conor Gilmartin, narr.) *Murther & Walking Spirits*

The best broadcloth isn't made of second-grade wool.
— (Conor Gilmartin, narr.) *Murther & Walking Spirits*

The bystanders get most of the splashed blood.
— (Conor Gilmartin, narr.) *Murther & Walking Spirits*

Everything, in time, begets its opposite.
— (Conor Gilmartin, narr.) *Murther & Walking Spirits*

You can't really form an opinion about somebody until you have seen the place where they live.
— (Dr. Jonathan Hullah, narr.) *The Cunning Man*

Don't miss a chance to acquire an ancestor.
— (Rhodri Cooper) *The Cunning Man*

While the funnies live, Aristophanes is never quite dead.
— (Brochwel Gilmartin) *The Cunning Man*

Learn to enjoy the pleasures of talk for talk's sake, without thinking you have to reshape your life every time a new idea comes along. — (Darcy Dwyer) *The Cunning Man*

Don't ask me to be consistent; it's the virtue of tiny minds.
— (Hugh McWearie) *The Cunning Man*

You can't use good means to reach a bad end.
— (Professor Idris Rowlands) *Fortune, My Foe*

Don't mistake sophisticated inexperience for innocence. Medusa was inexperienced, I suppose, before she turned her first man to stone; but the power and the urge were in her. — (Professor Idris Rowlands) *Fortune, My Foe*

Wholesome fruit doesn't grow on a cankered tree.
— (Nicholas Hayward) *Fortune, My Foe*

One can pay too dear for unity of any kind.
— (The Hon. Thomas Stewart) *At My Heart's Core*

When the east wind sweeps aside the toga we find that our idols have feet of clay. — (Richard Roberts) *A Jig for the Gypsy*

The world's like a man that's always bitin' on a sore tooth to see if it hurts as much as he thought it did a minute ago.
— (Conjuror Jones) *A Jig for the Gypsy*

There is no tyranny like that of organized virtue.
— (Count Fontenac) *Hope Deferred*

Not being serious is a civilized luxury.
— (The Shaman) *Question Time*

We all pay a price for what we have and what we are.
— (The Shaman) *Question Time*

Charisma embraces; style excludes. — (Arnak) *Question Time*

In important things there is no public or private. The flaw within becomes the flaw without, because public matters are the mirrors in which we see private matters.
— (The Shaman) *Question Time*

There is no romance so potent as the belief that one can get rid of one's past. — (A Herald) *Question Time*

Refinement must be made upon heavy ore, not upon cobwebs. — *The Mirror of Nature*

Be very careful of what you greatly desire, in your inmost heart, because the chances are very strong that you will get it, in one form or another. But it will never be just the way you expected. — *One Half of Robertson Davies*

There has been a widespread notion that the secret of elegance is austerity. Of course, in our saner moments we all know that the secret of elegance is taste. Austerity is what happens when people dare not trust their taste.
— *One Half of Robertson Davies*

We are not supposed to smell people, and millions of dollars are spent on various devices to kill human smell, either at its source, or in the nose of the proximate companion. But to the aroused, the truly curious, the enchanted, or the enchained, is there any better revealer of truth than a smell?
— (Conor Gilmartin, narr.) *Murther & Walking Spirits*

Of what use is an Establishment figure if he does not look like an Establishment figure? — *One Half of Robertson Davies*

I think that the familiar and basic things demand constant repetition, in an age when familiar and basic things are so often cast aside, as if we had outlived them.
— *One Half of Robertson Davies*

The indiscretion of yesterday is the rich feeding of today.
— *One Half of Robertson Davies*

A parody is a compliment; nobody troubles to mock what nobody takes seriously. — *One Half of Robertson Davies*

Innocence preserved too long sours into ignorance.
— *One Half of Robertson Davies*

Let us not equate the unknown with the not-worth-knowing. — *A Voice from the Attic*

A concept of obscenity appears to be as necessary to one's view of life as a concept of purity. — *A Voice from the Attic*

Gloom always confers prestige on the gloomy.
— *A Voice from the Attic*

Better a bad dream than no dream at all.
— *The Diary of Samuel Marchbanks*

Gardening is an undemocratic pursuit. Somebody crawls through the flowerbeds, weeding and grovelling like the beasts that perish; somebody else strolls in the cool of the evening, smelling the flowers. There is the garden-lord and the garden-serf. When we are all socialists, gardens will vanish from the earth. — *The Diary of Samuel Marchbanks*

Irrational dread is the scourge of our time.
— *The Diary of Samuel Marchbanks*

November is a month to breed pessimists.
— *The Diary of Samuel Marchbanks*

Much modern housing would be better called kennelling.
— *The Table Talk of Samuel Marchbanks*

When I argue with someone who scorns logic, and even reason, I have to depend on my talent for abuse if I hope to win. — *The Table Talk of Samuel Marchbanks*

People talk about evil frivolously . . . it's a way of diminishing its power, or seeming to do so. To talk about evil as if it were just waywardness or naughtiness is very stupid and trivial. Evil is the reality of at least half the world.
— (Jurgen Lind) *World of Wonders*

The longevity of nuisances is one of Nature's inexplicable jokes. — *Samuel Marchbanks' Almanack*

What evidence have we that a fox is clever? When chased it runs away, and makes better time in country it knows than a dog does. Is that clever? But a fox looks clever, and with animals as with humans, that is more than half the battle.
— *Samuel Marchbanks' Almanack*

Moderation in eating and drinking is to be avoided for as long as possible, as it is a great vexation while it is going on, and disposes you to regretful recollections when you are living on crackers and boiled milk.

— *Samuel Marchbanks' Almanack*

You are not supposed to kick the underdog, but it's perfectly okay for the underdog to bite you. One of the insoluble injustices of society. — (Simon Darcourt) *The Lyre of Orpheus*

Money

Money, it is often said, does not bring happiness; it must be added, however, that it makes it possible to support unhappiness with exemplary fortitude. — *Tempest-Tost*

Money alone can't hurt you. If you're a fool, or if you haven't any talent, or not enough, it will influence the special way in which you go to the devil. Money is a thing you have to control; it must play the part in your life that you allot to it, and it must never become the star turn. But take it from me, too much money is less harmful than too little. Wealth tends to numb feeling and nibble at talent, but poverty coarsens feeling and chokes talent.

— (Sir Benedict Domdaniel) *A Mixture of Frailties*

Does money change the essential man?
— (David Staunton, narr.) *The Manticore*

Wealth takes a man out of the middle class, unless he made all the money himself.
— (David Staunton, narr.) *The Manticore*

Simple people seem to think that if a family has money, every member dips what he wants out of some ever-replenished bag that hangs, perhaps, by the front door.
— (David Staunton, narr.) *The Manticore*

The rich man differed from the ordinary man only in that he had a wider choice, and that one of his dangerous choices was a lightly disguised slavery to the source of his wealth. — (Boy Staunton) *The Manticore*

Money's something you shove around, like electricity.
— (Arthur Cornish) *The Rebel Angels*

The paradox of money is that when you have lots of it you can manage life quite cheaply. Nothing so economical as being rich. — (John Parlabane) *The Rebel Angels*

Money illiteracy is as restrictive as any other illiteracy.
— (James McRory, Francis Cornish's grandfather) *What's Bred in the Bone*

There is no business so neurotic, fanciful, scared of its own shadow, and downright loony as the money business.

— (Arthur Cornish) *What's Bred in the Bone*

Banking is like religion: you have to accept certain rather dicey things simply on faith, and then everything else follows in marvellous logic.

— (Mrs. Arthur Cornish) *What's Bred in the Bone*

Scholars and artists have no morals whatever about grants of money. They'd take it from a house of child prostitution.

— (Simon Darcourt) *What's Bred in the Bone*

Comparatively few people know what a million dollars actually is. To the majority it is a gaseous concept, swelling or decreasing as the occasion suggests. In the minds of politicians, perhaps more than anywhere, the notion of a million dollars has this accordion-like ability to expand or contract; if they are disposing of it, the million is a pleasing sum, reflecting warmly upon themselves; if somebody else wants it, it becomes a figure of inordinate size, not to be compassed by the rational mind. — *What's Bred in the Bone*

Money is one of the two or three primary loyalties. You might forgive a man for trifling with a political cause, but not with your money, especially money that Chance has sent your way. — (Francis Cornish) *What's Bred in the Bone*

One does not restore a great fortune by shrinking from risks. – (The Countess) *What's Bred in the Bone*

The possession of wealth brings responsibilities; woe to the wealthy who seek to avoid them. – *The Lyre of Orpheus*

If a bank knew nothing except what comes to it from official sources it wouldn't last long. The readiness with which the mortgage money is repaid is in itself enough to arouse suspicion. The only people who pay up so readily, so often before the due date, are either the small group of the scrupulously honest – who probably don't go in for mortgages anyway – and those who don't want investigations or questions. – (Dr. Jonathan Hullah, narr.) *The Cunning Man*

Money, especially in very large quantities, is so much more desirable than the average young woman that no man of real wisdom would hesitate for an instant between the two. – *The Diary of Samuel Marchbanks*

Money will not bring happiness to a man who has no capacity for happiness, but neither will the possession of a woman who has no more brains than himself. But money will greatly increase the happiness of a man who is already happy (like me). – *The Diary of Samuel Marchbanks*

Morality

Moral causes, good and bad, may shout in the ears of men; aesthetic causes have lost the fight as soon as they begin to be strident. — *A Voice from the Attic*

Mind your economics, and your morals will take care of themselves. — *The Table Talk of Samuel Marchbanks*

Motherhood

It's a wise child that knows his father, but it's one child in a million who knows his mother. They're a mysterious mob, mothers. — (Ruth Nibsmith) *What's Bred in the Bone*

There is a whole large class of society — called children — to whom mothers are not women, but inescapable appendages, sometimes dear, sometimes not, and never full human beings but supporting players in their own intense drama. — (Dr. Jonathan Hullah, narr.) *The Cunning Man*

Music

Music is like wine; the less people know about it, the sweeter they like it. – (Humphrey Cobbler) *A Mixture of Frailties*

Purcell! What a genius! And lucky, too. Nobody has ever thought to blow him up into a God-like Genius, like poor old Bach, or a Misunderstood Genius, like poor old Mozart, or a Wicked and Immoral Genius, like poor old Wagner. Purcell is just a nice, simple Genius, rollicking happily through Eternity. The boobs and the gramophone salesmen and the music hucksters haven't discovered him yet and please God they never will. Kids don't peck and mess at little scraps of Purcell for examinations. Arthritic organists don't torture Purcell in chapels and tin Bethels all over the country on Sundays, while the middle classes are pretending to be holy. Purcell is still left for people who really like music. – (Humphrey Cobbler) *Tempest-Tost*

Music is a serious business. You may publish collections of literary oddities, but nobody wants musical oddities.
– (Humphrey Cobbler) *Leaven of Malice*

That's what music used to be for, you know – to capture the beauty and delight that people found in life. But then the Romantics came along and turned it all upside down; they made music a way of churning up emotions in people that they hadn't felt before. Music ceased to be a distillment of life and became, for a lot of people, a substitute for life – a substitute for a sea-voyage, or the ecstasies of sainthood, or being raped by a cannibal king, or even for an hour with a psychoanalyst or a good movement of the bowels. And a whole class of people arose who thought themselves music-lovers, but who were really sensation-lovers. Not that I'm a hundred per cent against the Romantics – just against the people who think that Romanticism is all there is of music. – (Sir Benedict Domdaniel) *A Mixture of Frailties*

Singers must eat, and there have been those among them who have eaten too much. As amorousness is the pastime of players of stringed instruments, and horse racing the relaxation of the brass section of the orchestra, so eating is the pleasure and sometimes the vice, of singers.
– *A Mixture of Frailties*

Old fiddles are like old people, they get cranky, and have to be coaxed, and sent to the spa, and have beauty treatments and all that.
– (Mamusia Laoutaro, mother of Maria Theotoky) *The Rebel Angels*

When I speak of the opera of my dreams, it is no forced elegance of words, I assure you, but the expression of what I believe music to be, and to be capable of expressing. For is not music a language? And of what is it the language? Is it not the language of the dream world, the world beyond thought, beyond the languages of Mankind? Music strives to speak to Mankind in the only possible language of this unseen world. — (ETAH in Limbo) *The Lyre of Orpheus*

Singers aren't picked up at the last minute. They're worse than hockey players; you have to get them under contract, or at least under written agreement, as far ahead as you can do it. — (Geraint Powell) *The Lyre of Orpheus*

Difficult winters make very great people, and great music. — (Dr. Gunilla Dahl-Soot) *The Lyre of Orpheus*

The life of a librettist is the life of a dog. Worse than the playwright, who may have to satisfy monsters of egotism with new scenes, new jokes, chances to do what they have done successfully before; but the playwright can, to some degree, choose the form of his scenes and his speeches. The librettist must obey the tyrant composer, whose literary taste may be that of a peasant, and who thinks of nothing but his music. Rightly so, of course. Opera is music, and all else must bow to that. But what sacrifices are demanded of the literary man! — (ETAH in Limbo) *The Lyre of Orpheus*

Music is too strongly the voice of emotion and it is not a good impersonator. — (ETAH in Limbo) *The Lyre of Orpheus*

The arpeggi must be deliberate, like pearls dropping in wine, not slithering like a fat woman slipping on a banana skin.
— (Dr. Gunilla Dahl-Soot, on playing the harp) *The Lyre of Orpheus*

What has Nature produced more totally ravishing than a beautiful, witty soprano?
— (Dr. Jonathan Hullah, narr.) *The Cunning Man*

A man likes his eye to be refreshed, but beauty perishes. A beautiful voice, however, goes on until death, and it can call up the ghost of vanished physical beauty more readily than any other spell. — *Samuel Marchbanks' Almanack*

Nature vs. Nurture

Nature and nurture are inextricable; only scientists and psychologists could think otherwise.
— (The Lesser Zadkiel) *What's Bred in the Bone*

Heredity is the old house we all have over our heads; environment is the junk we put in it. — (Fred Lewis) *Hunting Stuart*

Opera

There is no such thing as enough money for opera.
— *A Mixture of Frailties*

Characters in opera are really just like ordinary people . . .
except that they show us their souls.
— (Dr. Gunilla Dahl-Soot) *The Lyre of Orpheus*

An opera has to have a foundation; something big, like
unhappy love, or vengeance, or some point of honour.
Because people like that, you know. There they sit, all those
stockbrokers and rich surgeons and insurance men, and
they look so solemn and quiet as if nothing would rouse
them. But underneath they are raging with unhappy love,
or vengeance, or some point of honour or ambition – all
connected with their professional lives. They go to *La
Bohème* or *La Triviata* and they remember some early affair
that might have been squalid if you weren't living it yourself; or they see *Rigoletto* and think how the chairman
humiliated them at the last board meeting; or they see
Macbeth and think how they would like to murder the
chairman and get his job. Only they don't think it; very
deep down they feel it, and boil it, and suffer it in the
primitive underworld of their souls. You wouldn't get them
to admit anything, not if you begged. Opera speaks to the

heart as no other art does, because it is essentially simple.
— (Dr. Gunilla Dahl-Soot) *The Lyre of Orpheus*

More operas have been spoiled by too much artistic conscience than have ever been glorified by genius.
— (Geraint Powell) *The Lyre of Orpheus*

The artists and artificers who are assembled to put an opera on the stage make up a closed society, and no one who is not of the elect may hope to penetrate it. There is no ill-will in this; it is simply that people deep in an act of creation take their whole lives with them into that act, and the world outside becomes shadowy until the act is completed, the regular schedule of performances established, and the strength of association somewhat relaxed.
— *The Lyre of Orpheus*

Nothing encourages self-esteem like success as a singer. And why not? If you can stir an audience to its depths with your A *altissimo*, what need you care for anything else?
— (ETAH in Limbo) *The Lyre of Orpheus*

That is the operatic problem; the singer must keep up a big head of steam while trying to appear secretive, or seductive, or consumptive. Some ingenious composer should write an opera about a group of people who were condemned by a

cruel god to scream all the time; it would be an instantaneous success, and a triumph of verisimilitude.
— *The Diary of Samuel Marchbanks*

There is a childlike, unsophisticated quality about opera which commands respect in this wicked world. All that hooting and hollering because somebody has pinched somebody else's girl, or killed the wrong man, or sold his soul to the devil! These are commonplaces in daily life (particularly the latter) and it is astonishing to hear them treated with so much noisy consideration.
— *The Table Talk of Samuel Marchbanks*

Philanthropy / Patronage

Great collectors and great connoisseurs are not always nice people. Great benefactors, however, are invariably and unquestionably nice. — (Simon Darcourt, narr.) *The Rebel Angels*

Benefaction means self-satisfaction, nine times out of ten. The guile and cunning that enable benefactors to get their hands on the dough make it almost impossible for them to relinquish it, at the hour of death.
— (Urquhart McVarish) *The Rebel Angels*

Why is it assumed that someone who has fine things is under an obligation to give them away?
— (Francis Cornish) *What's Bred in the Bone*

Caution and non-intervention are the arthritis of patronage. — (Arthur Cornish) *The Lyre of Orpheus*

I know a lot about patronage because I've seen it in the university. Either you exploit, or you are exploited. Either you demand the biggest slice of the pie for yourself, and get a gallery, or a theatre, or whatever it may be, named after you, and insist that people put up your portrait in the foyer, and toady to you, and listen to whatever you have to say with bated breath, or else you are simply the moneybags.
— (Simon Darcourt) *The Lyre of Orpheus*

A patron has one of two courses: he may dominer and spoil the broth by insisting on too much salt or pepper; or he may simply do what God has enabled him to do, and that is to pay, pay, pay! — (ETAH in Limbo) *The Lyre of Orpheus*

An art patron today is a victim. The artists will crucify him and mock him and caricature him and strip him naked, if he hasn't got the drop on them from the start. Only when the Medici or the Esterhazys had their heel on the artist's neck did it work. Admit artists to equality and the jig's up.

Because they don't believe in equality. Only in their own superiority. — (Claude Applegarth, critic) *The Lyre of Orpheus*

Until you've tried it, you can have no idea of how hard it is to give away money. Intelligently, that's to say.
— (Arthur Cornish) *The Lyre of Orpheus*

All patrons are mocked behind their backs; it is a way artists have of maintaining self-respect.
— (Dr. Jonathan Hullah, narr.) *The Cunning Man*

Philosophy

Most adolescents are destructive, I suppose, but the worst are certainly those who justify what they do with a half-baked understanding of somebody's philosophy.
— (Liesl) *World of Wonders*

Sentimentalism is the philosophy of boobs.
— *A Voice from the Attic*

This is one of the great injustices of the world. A big man is always accused of gluttony, whereas a wizened or osseous man can eat like a refugee at every meal, and no one ever notices his greed. I have seen runts who never weighed more than ninety-six pounds when soaking wet outeat two-hundred-pounders, and poke fun at the fat man even as they licked their plates and sucked the starch out of their napkins. No wonder fat men are philosophers; they are forced to it. — *The Table Talk of Samuel Marchbanks*

Poetry

If a poet and a storyteller is both good, and dead, he may be considered the equal or even the superior of ordinary, decent, successful men; but so long as he has the bad taste to remain alive the question will always be in dispute, and the odds will always be heavily against him.
— (Mr. Edwin Cantwell) *At My Heart's Core*

Beginners at poetry . . . must choose rhyme or reason: they can't have both. — (Aristophontes) *Eros at Breakfast*

Even a terrible poet may hit on a truth. Even the blind pig sometimes finds the acorn.
— (Simon Darcourt) *The Lyre of Orpheus*

Politics

The first duty of a political party is to gain power.
— (Sir John Jebson) *A Jig for the Gypsy*

Politics is the art of the possible. — (Marge) *Question Time*

No country can hope to rise above mediocrity if it lacks the mystique of the courage, the humour, and also the cunning and roguery of its people. — (A Herald) *Question Time*

Give a [political] party its own way and it may rule very well. — (The Minister for External Affairs) *Question Time*

If a man were to sing in the street he would probably end up in jail; if he sang at his work the efficiency expert would ask him to come to his office for a frank talk. The way to impress your boss is to look glum all the time. He may mistake this for intelligence and give you a raise. The same holds true in politics: he who laughs is lost.
— *The Diary of Samuel Marchbanks*

I am a democrat, but the idea that a gang of anybodies may override the opinion of one expert is preposterous nonsense. Only individuals think; gangs merely throb.
— *The Diary of Samuel Marchbanks*

Many a man who has had a taste of acting takes to politics. The critics are less severe toward politicians than toward those who pursue the player's art in its more demanding form. — *Samuel Marchbanks' Almanack*

Rhetoric is only base when base men use it.
— (Simon Darcourt) *The Lyre of Orpheus*

Psychology

We've had psychology and we've had sociology and we're still just where we were for all practical purposes.
— (Simon Darcourt, narr.) *The Rebel Angels*

Jung is insistent on a particular type of development in the mind of anyone who meets the problems of life successfully; it is the change, the alteration of viewpoint, that transformation of aims and ambitions, that overtakes everybody somewhere in the middle of life. In women this change is physiological as well as mental, and consequently it has always been a matter of common observation. But in men the change is an intellectual and spiritual one of profound consequence. — *One Half of Robertson Davies*

Those to whom virtue is a luxury, dream of virtue. The aspirations of the psyche, and daily reality, are not identical.
— *One Half of Robertson Davies*

We all stand much nearer to unreason than we suppose.
— *One Half of Robertson Davies*

Quotations

I feed my fires with quotations.
— (Conor Gilmartin, narr.) *Murther & Walking Spirits*

The fake profundities of dead politicians, the treacly outpourings of fifth-rate poets, the moonlit nonsense of minor essayists – this junk makes up the bulk of most quotation books. — *Samuel Marchbanks' Almanack*

I love Latin quotations. I suspect that nobody ever said anything in Latin which was above the level of barbershop philosophy, but it has a wondrous sonority.
— *Samuel Marchbanks' Almanack*

Reading

Reading is a form of indulgence, like eating and smoking. Some men smoke heavily and some drink heavily; I read heavily, and sometimes I have the most awful hangovers.
— *The Diary of Samuel Marchbanks*

We do not read to make ourselves cultured, but to nourish our souls. Real culture is the evidence, not the reality, of the fully realized spirit. — *One Half of Robertson Davies*

Reading inexpert writing is deeply exhausting. It is like listening to bad music. — *One Half of Robertson Davies*

If you want to know and feel what a genius knows and feels, you must be a reader first, and a critic a very long way afterward. — *One Half of Robertson Davies*

It has long been a contention of mine that if you truly value a book you should read it when you are the age the author was when he wrote it. — *One Half of Robertson Davies*

Only people with no taste shun reading which is not in the highest taste; the true reader has favourites whose faults and deficiencies are obvious, but whose virtues are highly individual and uncommon. — *One Half of Robertson Davies*

To read a few novels written a century or more ago is not to drop our bucket very far into that deep Well of Time from which we may, if we choose, drink deeply. Nevertheless, it is a beginning, and wisdom is no more likely to be confined to the remote, the primordial past, than to the age in which we live. To sup the waters of even a century past may bring a change of vision. — *A Voice from the Attic*

End-gaining is one of the curses of our nervously tense, intellectually flabby civilization. In reading, as in all arts, it is the means, and not the end, which gives delight and brings true reward. — *A Voice from the Attic*

Every kind of prose has its own speed, and the experienced reader knows it as a musician knows Adagio from Allegro. — *A Voice from the Attic*

The reader must be satisfied; a fine style, a lively plot, interesting characters are of little avail if the book does not persuade the reader that the writer has been honest with him, and such honesty demands a sincere revelation of the writer's mind and heart. *A Voice from the Attic*

Surely if we possess the curiosity, the free mind, the belief in good taste, and the belief in the human race which characterize the humanist, we can choose the books we read on personal grounds, without experiencing unsettling sensations of eccentricity. — *A Voice from the Attic*

Revolution

Revolution is a city flower; it does not flourish in the country. — (Conor Gilmartin, narr.) *Murther & Walking Spirits*

Revolutions never change anything that matters; they merely put power in new hands, and the new masters have to serve their apprenticeship to civilization, like the rulers they have overthrown. — (Nicholas Hayward) *Fortune, My Foe*

The only revolutions that make any real difference to the world are revolutions in the hearts of individual men.
— (Nicholas Hayward) *Fortune, My Foe*

Rebellions against the codes of society begin at the top, not at the bottom. Stir the bottom and you get nothing but mud. — (Ronnie Fitzalan) *At the Gates of the Righteous*

Science

A life given to science had leached all belief out of him in things unseen, of heights and depths immeasurable.
– (Simon Darcourt, narr.) *The Rebel Angels*

The pride of science encourages us to this terrible folly and darkness of scorning the past.
– (Professor Mukadassi) *The Rebel Angels*

Science, which seems to offer certainty, is the superstition of ignorant multitudes.
– (Conor Gilmartin, narr.) *Murther & Walking Spirits*

One of the defects of the scientific viewpoint is that it leaves no room in life for poetry. – (Charlie Iredale) *The Cunning Man*

I am a creature of my time in that I fully understand that persons of merely aesthetic bias and training, like myself, should be silent in the presence of men of science, who know best about everything. – *One Half of Robertson Davies*

Science is the theology of our time, and like the old theology it's a muddle of conflicting assertions.
– (Simon Darcourt) *What's Bred in the Bone*

Self-pity

A little self-pity, I have always found, is very agreeable, so long as one keeps it to oneself. — *The Cunning Man*

I wonder why people are so down on self-pity? It is a cheap, agreeable amusement, requiring no elaborate equipment, like golf or polo. It imparts a pleasing melancholy to the countenance and a note of gentle charm to the voice. Most people despise self-pity in others because it makes them slightly uncomfortable which is a selfish reason for disapproving of anything. But I have always found that there is nothing like a good wallow in self-pity when my spirits are low, and I do not grudge to others an indulgence which has given me so much harmless pleasure.
— *The Table Talk of Samuel Marchbanks*

Self-respect

One derides one's long-lost self at the cost of some self-respect. — *One Half of Robertson Davies*

One does not take risks with the source of one's self-respect.
— *Tempest-Tost*

Self-righteousness

Self-righteousness is bound to be a characteristic of colonizing peoples; a grabber always wants moral backing when he grabs. If the grabber is an aristocrat in feeling, he justifies his grabbing on the simple ground that he is the stronger and therefore the superior, and that what he can seize he will hold. — *One Half of Robertson Davies*

Sex

Man is the only creature to know love as a complex emotion: man is also, in the whole of Nature, the only creature to turn sex into a hobby.
— (Professor Roberta Burns) *The Rebel Angels*

The value of virginity depends on whose it is; for trivial people, it is no doubt trivial.
— (Maria Theotoky) *The Rebel Angels*

Man is the only creature to have made a hobby and a fetish of Sex, and the bed is the great playpen of the world.
— *The Lyre of Orpheus*

Sex is an instinct, and for some people it seems to be the supreme pleasure, but what can you build on it? Forty or fifty years of marriage? No, that means truth and loyalty, when sex has become an old song.

— (Rhodri Cooper) *Murther & Walking Spirits*

Why do people so quickly get down to sex when they talk about sin, and why does it seem to be a thing of the darkness? — (Dr. Jonathan Hullah, narr.) *The Cunning Man*

In a real union sex becomes just another kind of happy talk, a song without words, a coming together which does not need explanations or considerations.

— (Dr. Jonathan Hullah, narr.) *The Cunning Man*

We [Jungians] have no quarrel with the Freudians, but we do not put the same stress on sexual matters as they do. Sex is very important, but if it were the single most important thing in life it would all be much simpler, and I doubt if mankind would have worked so hard to live far beyond the age when sex is the greatest joy. It is a popular delusion, you know, that people who live very close to nature are the great ones for sex. Not a bit. You live with primitives and you find out the truth. People wander around naked and nobody cares — not even an erection or a wiggle of the hips. That is because their society does not give them the brandy of

Romance, which is the great drug of our world. When sex is on the program they sometimes have to work themselves up with dances and ceremonies to get into the mood for it, and then of course they are very active. But their important daily concern is with food. You know, you can go for a lifetime without sex and come to no special harm. Hundreds of people do so. But you go for a day without food and the matter becomes imperative. — (Dr. J. von Haller) *The Manticore*

Shakespeare

Age cannot wither Shakespeare, but it stales his parodists with astonishing rapidity. — *A Voice from the Attic*

Cheap romance is exclusive; it shuts out all that is not pretty and flattering in life. Shakespearean romance, and all great romance, is inclusive, embracing, and understanding all of life. — *Renown at Stratford*

Given taste, you can then go as far as you like with your big stage effects. Hundreds of people milling about if you like. Fill the stage with horses and dogs. Pageantry in a big way. Make it complex! Let it fill the eye! Let it be enriched, bejewelled, Byzantine! The parrot-cry that simplicity is one with good taste comes from people who cannot trust their taste in anything which is not simple. Shakespeare demands all the opulence that we can give him!

— (Humphrey Cobbler) *Tempest-Tost*

Sin

Let my sin be Sin or it loses all stature.

— (John Parlabane) *The Rebel Angels*

Puritans enjoy sin more than ordinary people; not only do they have the fun of doing whatever it may be that is wrong, but they have the fun of self-accusation, repentance, penitence, and similar emotional binges.

— *The Table Talk of Samuel Marchbanks*

Skepticism

If one regards oneself as a skeptic, it is a good plan to have occasional doubts about one's skepticism too.

— *One Half of Robertson Davies*

I, as a skeptic, am committed to non-belief in everything, including my most cherished philosophical ideas.
— (John Parlabane) *The Rebel Angels*

Snobbery

A little snobbery, like a little politeness, oils the wheels of daily life. — *Tempest-Tost*

In my experience snobbery sometimes means no more than a rejection of what is truly inferior.
— (Dr. Jonathan Hullah, narr.) *The Cunning Man*

I'm not faddy about wine; the best will do.
— (The town mouse) *A Masque of Aesop*

It is a widespread belief that a truly critical mind exists in a constant state of high-toned irascibility.
— *A Voice from the Attic*

Snobbery, like every other social attitude, takes its character from those who practise it. The snob is supposedly a mean creature, delighting in slight and trivial distinctions. But is the man who bathes every day a snob because he does not seek the company of the one-bath-a-week, one-shirt-a-week, one-pair-of-clean-drawers-a-week, one-pair-of-socks-a-week man? Must the gourmet embrace the barbarian whose idea of a fine repast is a hamburger made from the flesh of fallen animals, and a tub of fries soaked in vinegar? Is the woman who wears a first-rate intaglio to be faulted because she thinks little of the woman whose fingers are loaded with fake diamonds? — (Conor Gilmartin, narr.) *Murther & Walking Spirits*

Soul

Chastity is having the body in the soul's keeping.
— (Sir Benedict Domdaniel) *A Mixture of Frailties*

A little terror, in my view, is good for the soul, when it is terror in the face of a noble object.
— (Dunstan Ramsay) *World of Wonders*

Souls are not fashionable, at present. People will listen with wondering acquiescence to scientific talk of such invisible entities as are said to be everywhere and very important, but they shy away from talk of souls. Souls have a bad name in the world of atomic energy. — *The Lyre of Orpheus*

The soul can't just exist as a sort of gas that makes us noble when we let it. The soul is something else: we have to lodge our souls somewhere and people project their souls, their energy, their best hopes – call it what you like – onto something. The two great carriers of soul are money and sex. There are lots of others: power, or security (that's a bad one), and of course art – and that's a good one.

— (Simon Darcourt) *The Lyre of Orpheus*

Spirituality

Has there ever, I wonder, been a period of history when so many people worked so hard, at such dull tasks, in order to maintain a quality of life which is better than anything the majority of mankind could have enjoyed in the past, but which is bought at the cost of unremitting work, economic complexity, lifelong burdens of debt, and an hysterical craving for more and costlier physical objects of a kind that can never requite the toil and servitude it takes to acquire them. In the midst of our heaped-up abundance of things made of metal and wires and plastic, we starve for the bread of the spirit. — *One Half of Robertson Davies*

Success

Failure I can endure; success I like but not too much. Mediocrity turns my stomach.
— (Dr. Gunilla Dahl-Soot) *The Lyre of Orpheus*

Do not be discouraged by lack of immediate success. Bernard Shaw flowered at seventeen, but nobody smelled him until he was forty. — *Samuel Marchbanks' Almanack*

Be most alert when most victorious, for though you may not hit your adversary when he is down, it is considered plucky in him to kick you. — *Samuel Marchbanks' Almanack*

Theatre

One of the nicest things about the professional theatre is that it is utterly undemocratic. If you aren't any good, you go. Or maybe that's real democracy.
— (Roscoe Forrester) *Tempest-Tost*

Nobody has ever written a great play on a Biblical theme. Milton couldn't pull it off. Even Ibsen steered clear of Holy Writ. There's something about it that defies dramatization.
— (Humphrey Cobbler) *Leaven of Malice*

The terrible truth is that feeling really does have to be learned. It comes spontaneously when one is in love, or when somebody important dies; but people like you and me — interpretative artists — have to learn also to recapture those feelings, and transform them into something which we can offer to the world in our performances.
— (Sir Benedict Domdaniel) *A Mixture of Frailties*

Theatre people have little reverence — except when they look in the mirror. — (ETAH in Limbo) *The Lyre of Orpheus*

I hate theatre where the audience is told to use its imagination. That's cheap. The audience lays down its good money to rent imagination from somebody who has more than they ever dreamed of.
— (Dulcy Ringgold) *The Lyre of Orpheus*

There are no great performances without great audiences, and this is the barrier that film and television, by their utmost efforts, cannot cross, for there can be no interaction between what is done, and those to whom it is done. Great theatre, great music-drama, is created again and again on both sides of the footlights. — *The Lyre of Orpheus*

Every playgoer is a psychologist. — (Chremes) *Eros at Breakfast*

A playwright should never answer his critics.
— Preface to *A Jig for the Gypsy*

The theatre is a house of dreams, in which audiences gather to share a dream that is presented to them by a group of artists who are particularly skilled in bodying forth dreams.
— *One Half of Robertson Davies*

A fine performance of a great play is one of the most compelling and rewarding experiences our culture provides, and it is also a highly sophisticated version of that experience of which anthropologists have written, where members of the tribe gather together to be told a great dream which is of importance to the tribe. — *One Half of Robertson Davies*

Poetry and the novel are encountered by the solitary reader, drawn apart from his fellows. But a play must make its effect immediately, in a short time, on a mixed audience whose attention must be seized and held from distraction, and that expects qualities for its money which do not trouble poetry or the novel.
— *The Mirror of Nature*

To be present in an audience is still, in our time, somewhat to condone the performance. We are claiming to be at one with the players as we do not need to admit to being at one with the poet or the novelist. — *The Mirror of Nature*

The theatre seldom goes against the spirit of the age, for it is the mirror of nature. — *The Mirror of Nature*

The scholar in the theatre is a pest, if he carries a burden of knowledge which is not balanced by any comparable creative ability. — *Renown at Stratford*

One of the joys of the theatre is that one may change allegiances immediately and without compunction.
— *Renown at Stratford*

Clothes which are merely modish are destructive of great drama, just as a method of speaking which is too much of one time and place is destructive to it.
— *Renown at Stratford*

The drama, in its finest flights, gives me a satisfaction, an elation and a recreation which makes the pleasures of the greatest music seem thin and chilly in comparison. Music is an intellectual extract of life; drama is life itself, raised to the highest pitch.
— *The Table Talk of Samuel Marchbanks*

War

When a war is over, the cleaning-up and the arranging, and the vengeance toward the vanquished, take just as much time and clashing of brains as the conflict itself.
— *What's Bred in the Bone*

Wars are national and international disasters, but everyone in a warring nation fights a war of his own and sometimes it cannot be decided whether he has won or lost.
— *What's Bred in the Bone*

The idea of being a soldier is a powerful archetype; take almost any man and put him in the Army and the archetype of the brutal and licentious soldiery will manifest itself and he will behave in a way that perhaps surprises himself.
— (Dr. Jonathan Hullah, narr.) *The Cunning Man*

Wisdom

We all subscribe thoughtlessly to many beliefs, the truth of which does not strike home to us until experience gives them reality. Wisdom may be rented, so to speak, on the experience of other people, but we buy it at an inordinate price before we make it our own forever. — *Leaven of Malice*

One must visit a wise man from time to time to discover what one already knows. — (Hugh McWearie) *The Cunning Man*

Our age has robbed millions of the simplicity of ignorance, and has so far failed to lift them to the simplicity of wisdom. — *A Voice from the Attic*

The merriment of wise men is not the uninformed, gross fun of ignorant men, but it has more kinship with that than with the pinched, frightened fun of those who are neither learned nor ignorant, gentle nor simple, bond nor free. The idea that a wise man must be solemn is bred and preserved among people who have no idea of what wisdom is, and can only respect whatever makes them feel inferior.
— *A Voice from the Attic*

It's a wise man who knows when to give his doubts a rest.
— (Sir John Jebson) *A Jig for the Gypsy*

Wisdom is the greatest possession in the world; money comes next; the intimate caresses of Hollywood stars come a long way down the list . . . — *The Diary of Samuel Marchbanks*

Wisdom is a variable possession. Every man is wise when pursued by a mad dog; fewer when pursued by a mad woman; only the wisest survive when attacked by a mad notion. — *Samuel Marchbanks' Almanack*

Women

I sometimes think a woman has no country; only a family.
— *What's Bred in the Bone*

It is hard on women to be looked on as mothers only.
— (Dr. J. von Haller) *The Manticore*

There used to be a widespread idea that women are very sensitive. My experience of them as clients, witnesses, and professional opponents had dispelled any illusions I might have had of that kind. — (David Staunton, narr.) *The Manticore*

A woman cannot live solely in the realm of her love; she must have a life of her own; she must shed light, as well as reflecting it. — *The Lyre of Orpheus*

So few women these days are up to their job as females. I think of starting a small school to teach girls the arts of enchantment. They certainly won't learn anything from their liberated sisters.
— (Simon Darcourt) *The Lyre of Orpheus*

Quiet girls, whom some men admire so much, always make me think of clocks that have run down. — *High Spirits*

To know when to be beautiful and when to be common-place is one of the great secrets of life, particularly for a woman. — (Count Fontenac) *Hope Deferred*

There is an ill-justified notion that women are peace-makers. — *What's Bred in the Bone*

By the mercy of God, no woman can be ruined more than once. After that, she's in the public domain.
— (Henry Benedict Stuart) *Hunting Stuart*

Many a one hath cast away her final worth when she hath cast away her servitude.
— (Sarah Macadam, wife of Prime Minister Macadam) *Question Time*

The idea that women are sympathetic is grossly overdone.
— *The Diary of Samuel Marchbanks*

The bitter truth about women is that their minds work precisely like those of men: the bitter truth about men is that they are too vain to admit it. — *Samuel Marchbanks' Almanack*

Chivalry . . . I think we have seen the last of it for a while on this earth. It can't live in a world of liberated women, and perhaps the liberation of women is worth the price it is certain to cost. But chivalry won't die easily or unnoticed;

banish chivalry from the world and you snap the main-spring of many lives. — (Dunstan Ramsay) *World of Wonders*

Writing

It's the classic problem of autobiography; it's inevitably life seen and understood backward. However honest we try to be in our recollections we cannot help falsifying them in terms of later knowledge, and especially in terms of what we have become. — (Roland Ingestree) *World of Wonders*

You can't make a novelist out of a philosopher.
— (Professor Clement Hollier) *The Rebel Angels*

There is a special frustration that afflicts authors when they cannot claim enough time for their own work.
— *The Lyre of Orpheus*

She had never been what I call a good writer. No serious regard for language.
— (Conor Gilmartin, narr.) *Murther & Walking Spirits*

Nobody but a fool wants to fail when he sets to work to write a novel, and it is the hope that he may succeed where others – in so many ways his better – have failed that keeps him going. *– A Voice from the Attic*

The difference between comedy and tragedy is less often one of theme than of the prevailing colour of the writer's mind. *– A Voice from the Attic*

Are there comic themes, or only comic writers – men whose quality of mind and means of expression are comic, without thereby being any less compassionate or understanding or profound than the writers of tragedy? *– A Voice from the Attic*

Belief in God and a good education are not enough to produce a good novel; only talent can do that, and where talent exists, it may produce the novel without either of the other aids. *– A Voice from the Attic*

The difference between the amateur autobiographer and the professional man of letters is that the former is concerned with self-approval, the latter with self-revelation. *A Voice from the Attic*

During the past century autobiography has added a new and undemanding pastime to old age. *– A Voice from the Attic*

A great writer must give us either great feeling from the heart or great wisdom from the head.
— *A Voice from the Attic*

If we want intelligent comment about writing and the temperament of writers, we are more likely to get it from writers themselves than from critics.
— *A Voice from the Attic*

Much bad art hides behind Christianity, for to criticize it on purely artistic grounds is to seem callous toward its inspiration; the Sistine Chapel and the fifty-cent chromo, the St. Matthew Passion and Moody and Sankey's hymns, Pilgrim's Progress and The Robe – to millions of people these seem more alike than unlike. To write about Christ is to disarm criticism and leave the way open for excesses which would not otherwise be tolerated. — *A Voice from the Attic*

If the writer of tragedy is not denied his fun, why should we deny the writer of comedy his gloom?
— *One Half of Robertson Davies*

Serious and tragic novelists are so often expected to write under the influence of some sort of religion, whereas comic novelists are not thought to have any such requirement. Such an attitude springs from the old, fallacious idea that joy and merriment are not religious feelings, whereas a miserable fate or a tragic life must carry with it some paraphernalia of the displeasure of God, or of the gods.

— *One Half of Robertson Davies*

Writers who are enclosed in a kingdom of this world do not have the big literary artillery, and when we have wearied of them, we are likely to turn again to the authors who, overtly or by implication, write as if man lived in the presence of a transcendent authority, and of an Adversary who sought to come between him and the light. — *One Half of Robertson Davies*

One of the burdensome parts of the writer's temperament, as I understand it, is that one feels quite strongly about all sorts of things that other people seem to be able to gloss over, and this can be wearisome and depleting.

— *One Half of Robertson Davies*

The writer is necessarily a man of feeling and intuition; he need not be a powerful original thinker.

— *One Half of Robertson Davies*

That realm of the Unconscious, which is the dwelling-place of so many demons and monsters, is also the home of the Muses, the abode of the angels. — *One Half of Robertson Davies*

The sense of comedy of a great writer is as important in understanding him as his sense of tragedy or pathos.
— *The Mirror of Nature*

Nobody keeps anything valuable in a safe any more. . . . Valuables are kept in banks. Manuscripts are kept in confused heaps on desks. — *The Table Talk of Samuel Marchbanks*

The proper corrective for the mental ills of the man who deals primarily in words is a brief spell of dealing with things; the contrariness and obduracy of such things as dirt, boxes, and old potato bags bring humility to the writer's heart . . . — *The Diary of Samuel Marchbanks*

I am a writer, a job in which advancing senility is rarely detectable. — *The Diary of Samuel Marchbanks*

Magic, not psychology, is the stuff of which great stories are made. — *The Table Talk of Samuel Marchbanks*

The man who writes only for the eye generally writes badly; the man who writes to be heard will write with some eloquence, some regard for the music of words, and will reach nearer to his reader's heart and mind.
— *The Table Talk of Samuel Marchbanks*

Even a mediocre writer may create one golden phrase.
— *Samuel Marchbanks' Almanack*

There are millions of people who think that writing, and painting, and music are things which their practitioners pick up in an idle hour; they have no conception of the demands these apparently trivial pastimes make upon those who are committed to them. — *Samuel Marchbanks' Almanack*

A writer should not take handouts from anybody, even his country. — *Samuel Marchbanks' Almanack*

Grants to authors are best confined to those who, by reason of age or misfortune, must have them, and public subventions are best confined to the performers, rather than the originators, of works of art. — *Samuel Marchbanks' Almanack*

Youth

Whom the gods hate they keep forever young.
— (Dunstan Ramsay, narr.) *Fifth Business*

Nobody changes so decisively that they lose all sense of the reality of their youth. — (Jurgen Lind) *World of Wonders*

One remembers one's youthful behaviour as nobody else does; one blushes for gaucheries nobody else has noticed.
— (Dr. Jonathan Hullah, narr.) *The Cunning Man*

In youth chance separates us from even the closest friends, and in the excitement of finding new ones we do not greatly notice the loss. — (Dr. Jonathan Hullah, narr.) *The Cunning Man*

The courage of youth has very strict limits.
— (Dr. Maria Clementina Sobieska) *Hunting Stuart*

A visit to a good barn is like a plunge into the fountain of youth. — *Samuel Marchbanks' Almanack*